IN THE GREEK TYCOON'S BED

They're dangerously handsome and
impossibly wealthy....

They're used to having it all....

The secluded beaches of their private
islands make the perfect setting for red-hot
seduction....

These Greek billionaires will stop at nothing
to bed their chosen mistresses—
women who find themselves powerless
to resist being pleasured....

IN THE GREEK TYCOON'S BED

*At the mercy of a ruthless
Mediterranean billionaire...*

CHANTELLE SHAW lives on the Kent coast, five minutes from the sea, and does much of her thinking about the characters in her books while walking on the beach. An avid reader from an early age, she found that school friends used to hide their books when she visited. But Chantelle would retreat into her own world, and she still writes stories in her head all the time.

Chantelle has been blissfully married to her own tall, dark and very patient hero for over twenty years, and has six children. She began to read Harlequin novels as a teenager, and throughout the years of being a stay-at-home mom to her brood, found romance fiction helped her to stay sane! Her aim is to write books that provide an element of escapism, fun and of course romance for the countless women who juggle work and a home life and who need their precious moments of "me" time.

She enjoys reading and writing about strong-willed, feisty women and even stronger-willed, sexy heroes. Chantelle is at her happiest when writing. She is particularly inspired while cooking dinner, which unfortunately results in a lot of culinary disasters! She also loves gardening, taking her very badly behaved terrier for walks and eating chocolate (followed by more walking—at least the dog is slim!).

THE GREEK TYCOON'S VIRGIN MISTRESS

CHANTELLE SHAW

~ IN THE GREEK TYCOON'S BED ~

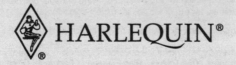

HARLEQUIN®

TORONTO • NEW YORK • LONDON
AMSTERDAM • PARIS • SYDNEY • HAMBURG
STOCKHOLM • ATHENS • TOKYO • MILAN • MADRID
PRAGUE • WARSAW • BUDAPEST • AUCKLAND

ISBN-13: 978-0-373-82081-8
ISBN-10: 0-373-82081-X

THE GREEK TYCOON'S VIRGIN MISTRESS

First North American Publication 2008.

www.eHarlequin.com

Printed in U.S.A.

THE GREEK TYCOON'S
VIRGIN MISTRESS

In memory of my mum, Gabrielle

CHAPTER ONE

THE dying rays of the sun glanced across the sandstone walls of Otterbourne House so that it appeared to glow like burnished gold. As Anna scrunched across the gravel drive she reached into her handbag for her compact, flipped open the lid and scrutinised her appearance in the mirror. Her career as a model and the 'face' of an international cosmetics company necessitated spending hours being made up, but in private she usually opted for a more natural look.

Tonight she'd gone for the full works. Her reflection revealed an exquisite mask of porcelain skin stretched taut over sharp cheekbones, the deep blue of her eyes emphasised by the careful application of a taupe-coloured shadow and her lips coated in chic, scarlet gloss.

On any other occasion, dinner with her closest friend Kezia Niarchou and her husband Nik at their home in the Hertfordshire countryside would have called for casual attire suitable for crawling around on the floor with her little godson Theo. But tonight was different and she looked the epitome of glamour in her black designer cocktail dress.

Goodbye, Anna—hello, Anneliese Christiansen, sophisticated supermodel, she thought derisively as she snapped the compact shut and took a deep breath. Ever since Kezia had dropped the bombshell that Nik's cousin Damon would be present at the dinner party, Anna's nerves had been on edge. Damon Kouvaris was something else and right now she wished he were somewhere else, preferably on the other side of the world.

'Fashionably late is one thing, but you're pushing it,' Kezia greeted good-naturedly when she opened the door and ushered Anna inside. 'Luckily it's a cold first course, but I've been detecting rumblings from the kitchen that Mrs Jessop's fretting about her *boeuf en croûte.*'

'I'm sorry, didn't you get my text? I had a flat tyre,' Anna murmured apologetically. 'Fortunately that young guy from the ground-floor flat fitted the spare for me.'

'I should hope so; you could hardly have jacked up the car in that dress. You look gorgeous but I'm curious to know who you're hoping to impress,' Kezia murmured softly, her eyes widening when Anna blushed. 'It couldn't be Damon by any chance, could it?'

'No, it could not,' Anna drawled, managing to affect just the right amount of lazy amusement in her voice. They had been as close as sisters since their first day at boarding-school and their friendship had weathered her parents' bitter divorce and Kezia's battle with leukaemia. The bond between them was unbreakable but some things were too personal to share, certainly her inexplicable fascination with Damon Kouvaris.

Nik's cousin's reputation as a ruthless businessman was almost as legendary as the rumours of his prowess in the bedroom. He was said to be a dynamic lover with an insatiable interest in sophisticated blondes and Anna had no intention of joining his list of conquests. Yet, to her extreme irritation, she had been unable to forget him these past two months.

The guests were assembled in the drawing room. She followed Kezia through the doorway and smiled warmly at the group of her most trusted friends.

'Anna, what can I get you to drink?' Nikos Niarchou strode across the room to greet her. Tall, dark and impossibly handsome, Nik had exchanged roles from jet-setting playboy to devoted husband and father without a backward glance. He dropped a light kiss on Anna's cheek but his gaze returned immediately to Kezia.

This was how marriage should be, Anna acknowledged hollowly, noting how Nik's dark eyes glowed with love for his wife. No man had ever looked at her with such tender adoration and she was aware of a faint pang of envy that she quickly suppressed. Kezia, more than anyone, deserved to be happy and Anna was genuinely delighted for her. It wasn't as if she had any great desire to sample the joys of matrimony anyway, she reminded herself. Her parents were both on their third attempts and she had no intention of following their rocky path down the aisle of nuptial bliss.

'I hear you had trouble with your car. You should have let us know earlier—I would have sent my driver to collect you,' Nik admonished lightly. 'You're almost as stubborn as my wife,' he added with a grin. 'Come and say hello to the others.'

There was no sign of Nik's cousin but Anna felt as tense as an overstrung bow when she greeted the other couples. It was instantly apparent that she was the only person present who did not have a partner. It wasn't an unusual occurrence—she had no one special in her life and at social engagements she usually relied on a select group of male models and actor friends to play the role of her escort.

Tonight, knowing she was among friends, she had come alone but now she wished she had brought one of her faithful band of chaperons. She could only pray that Damon was accompanied by one of his numerous lovers because the idea of sitting next to him throughout dinner caused a peculiar feeling in the pit of her stomach.

For a second she seriously considered asking for a large gin and tonic to settle her nerves. She was being ridiculous, she told herself sternly as she followed Nik to the bar and requested her usual choice of iced water. Since Kezia's marriage, Otterbourne had become a second home to her and she had been looking forward to spending a pleasant evening. No way would she allow Nik's spine-tinglingly sexy cousin to unsettle her.

Forcing herself to relax, she was drawn into conversation with the other guests and her tension eased. Perhaps Damon wasn't here after all? she brooded, dismayed by the sharp pang of disappointment the thought evoked. As the head of Kouvaris Construction, he took a personal interest in every element of his business and she knew he led a hectic lifestyle travelling between the company's various projects. Maybe he had been called away to deal with some crisis, as he had when she had first met him on Nik's private Aegean island, Zathos, two months earlier.

The conversation was light and entertaining and she gave a peal of laughter when one of her friends recounted an amusing anecdote, but a sudden prickling sensation on her skin set the fine hairs on the back of her neck on end. Some innate sixth sense warned her she was being watched and she turned her head sharply as a figure appeared in the doorway leading to the terrace.

Damon!

Instantly she was overwhelmed by his exceptional height and the formidable width of shoulders. Silhouetted against the evening sunshine he appeared so muscular and powerful that for a moment she could almost believe he were a figure from Greek mythology. Angrily she gave herself a mental shake and sought to tear her eyes from him, but he trapped her gaze and she swallowed at the brooding sexuality reflected in his midnight dark depths.

'Ah, Damon, there you are,' Nik said with a smile. 'You met Anna on Zathos, at Theo's christening, if you remember.'

'I haven't forgotten,' came the dry response. 'It's good to see you, Anna.'

His voice was low-pitched and melodious, reminding Anna of the sound of a bow being drawn lovingly across the strings of a cello. His Greek accent was heavily pronounced. Her name had never before sounded so sensual and her reaction was instant. A quiver ran the length of her spine and she affected a brief, impersonal smile.

'Mr Kouvaris! How nice to meet you again.' She extended her hand in formal greeting and gasped when he entwined his fingers through hers to draw her close. Before she had time to react he lowered his head and brushed his lips first on one cheek and then the other, the touch of his mouth on her skin causing goose bumps to cover every inch of her body.

Her career as a model meant that she frequently travelled abroad and was accustomed to the continental greeting, but her instant and overwhelming awareness of Damon caused hectic colour to stain her cheeks. Abruptly she stepped back, her heart racing as warmth coursed through her veins. Her head was spinning as if she had drunk a whole bottle of champagne and she inhaled sharply, desperate to compose herself.

'I hope you are well, Mr Kouvaris?' She managed the polite enquiry through gritted teeth and felt a flash of irritation when his mouth curved into a slow smile that told her he was well aware of her reaction to him.

'Very well, thank you,' he assured her gravely. 'My name is Damon—in case you've forgotten,' he added in a tone that spoke plainly of his confidence that she had not. 'I think we can dispense with formality, don't you, Anna? After all, we're practically family.'

Anna's brows lifted fractionally. 'I'm not sure how you've reached that conclusion,' she drawled, grateful that the years of practice at masking her emotions ensured she sounded cool and aloof, despite the erratic thud of her heart.

'I'm Nik's cousin and you are his wife's closest friend. According to Kezia, the two of you are practically sisters.' Damon had moved without her being aware of it and Anna discovered that she had been manoeuvred into a corner, slightly apart from the other guests. He was much too close for comfort. Her eyes were drawn to his face, noting the contrast between his dark olive skin and his brilliant white teeth revealed when he smiled at her.

He wasn't handsome in the conventional sense and certainly did not share the perfect features of the male models she worked with. With his strong, slightly hooked nose, heavy black brows and square jaw, Damon reminded her of a boxer who had gone several rounds with a forceful opponent. The formidable width of his shoulders and his powerful physique added to his air of raw, earthy masculinity but it was his mouth, full lipped and innately sensual, that captured Anna's attention.

His kiss would be no gentle seduction, she acknowledged faintly, moistening her suddenly dry lips with the tip of her tongue. Damon exuded a degree of sexual magnetism that warned her he would demand total submission. He would be an uninhibited, possessive lover and would use his mouth as an instrument of sensual torture that would be impossible to resist.

Where on earth had that thought come from? she wondered frantically, dragging her gaze from his face to focus on his crisp white shirt. She was tall but he dwarfed her and she felt intimidated by his sheer size, the latent strength of his broad, muscular chest.

'So, Anna—' his voice caressed every syllable of her name

'—you look stunning. You've been abroad.' His eyes skimmed over her, noting her soft golden tan. 'South Africa, I understand.'

'Yes, but how did you—?' She broke off with an impatient shrug. Kezia must have told him—it was hardly a state secret after all—but the knowledge that he must have asked about her was unsettling. No wonder Kezia had teased her about him when she'd first arrived. She just hoped her friend wasn't harbouring any hopes about matchmaking.

'I discovered your whereabouts from your agency,' he admitted without a hint of contrition, amusement glimmering in his dark eyes when she rounded on him indignantly.

'Why?' she demanded crossly, unable to disguise her confusion at his apparent interest. He hadn't bothered to hide his faint disdain of her chosen profession when Nik had first introduced them on Zathos. Indeed, she'd gained the distinct impression that he believed her to be a brainless bimbo, and the knowledge still stung. 'The agency wouldn't have given out information like that to just anyone,' she snapped.

'They gave it to me. But I am not "just anyone",' he stated with breathtaking arrogance, 'I am Damon Kouvaris, and once I'd convinced them that I was a personal friend of yours they were most helpful.'

'But you're not. We barely know each other. We've only met once, and the fact that we danced together at our godson's christening does not make us bosom buddies.'

The moment she'd uttered the word bosom, Anna could have cut her tongue out. Her chest was heaving with the force of her emotions. She felt Damon's gaze slide over her and was mortified to feel her breasts swell and tighten beneath the sheer black silk of her dress.

'There you are, you see. Already you've mentioned the unbreakable link between us. Theo, our godson,' Damon elucidated when she stared at him in confusion. 'He's one very good reason why we should take the opportunity to get to know one another better. You could even say it is our duty, *ne?*'

He was laughing at her, damn him, she realised furiously. She'd been thrilled when Kezia had asked her to be godmother to her little adopted son. It was an honour she had vowed to undertake to the best of her ability and she had travelled to Zathos, eager to meet her fellow godparent.

Unfortunately Nik's disturbingly sexy cousin was nothing like the sort of guardian she had imagined Kezia would have chosen for her son. Damon was Nik's choice, her friend had explained. She didn't know him that well but Nik thought a lot of him and, as far as Kezia was concerned, that settled the matter. Anna had been forced to swallow her doubts but she couldn't imagine that Damon, with his rugged good looks and magnetic charm, had any interest whatsoever in children.

His interest in women, however, was not in doubt. He possessed a blatant, simmering sexuality that was an almost primitive force. One glance from his dark, flashing eyes was enough to render any woman weak at the knees. Anna knew this from experience; hers had practically given way when Nik had first introduced them and now she was aware of the same trembling in her limbs as she faced the full onslaught of Damon's potent charm.

'Sorry to interrupt, but if we don't go in to dinner Mrs Jessop is likely to spontaneously-combust.' Kezia's light tone was a welcome release from the tension that gripped Anna and she expelled her breath sharply.

Damon stood aside and smiled at their hostess. 'Then we must come at once,' he said in the deep, gravelly voice that sent a delicious shiver down Anna's spine. 'I note that you don't have a partner this evening, Anna,' he murmured silkily. 'I, too, am alone and it would give me great pleasure to escort you to dinner.'

It was a perfectly reasonable request, Anna acknowledged, giving him a tight smile and allowing him to draw her arm through his. But she didn't feel reasonable. Damon unsettled her so that she felt edgy and irritable and yet at the same time wildly alive, her senses heightened to an unbearable degree.

When they followed the other guests into the dining room she was conscious of the brush of his thigh against hers and her body clenched. What was happening to her? She was Anneliese Christiansen. Her nickname of Ice Princess by certain elements of the press was well-deserved. Nobody got under her guard—ever—and it was infuriating to find that this arrogant, presumptuous Greek had the ability to shake her equilibrium.

No more, she vowed when Damon drew out a chair for her to sit down, before taking his place next to her at the table. She caught the tang of his aftershave, a spicy, exotic concoction that set her senses racing and it took considerable will-power to unfold her napkin and smile at him with an air of self-assurance she did not feel.

He was too pushy, too confident—she would take great delight in countering his outrageous flirting with the cool indifference that she had perfected to an art form, she decided firmly.

The first course was a delicious seafood salad. Plump, pink prawns nestled on a bed of crisp lettuce, dressed with a delicate sauce that stirred Anna's taste buds. She'd eaten nothing since her usual breakfast of yoghurt and fruit and had spent the day in a state of pent up tension at the thought of meeting Damon again. Now she forced herself to relax and speared a prawn with her fork.

'Did you enjoy your trip to South Africa? It boasts some spectacular scenery.'

The sensual resonance of his voice curled around her so that she found it suddenly hard to swallow. 'It was a working trip and there was no time for sightseeing,' she replied politely. As usual, the trip had been a whirl of airport lounges and hotel vestibules with a few days on the beach where she had been too busy modelling a range of swimwear to take more than a cursory interest in her surroundings.

'That's a pity. The wild flowers on the veldt are stunning at this time of the year. Do you often work to such a tight schedule?' Damon enquired lightly, his tone plainly implying that he did not consider standing around in a se-lection of designer frocks hard work. He'd made other, faintly disparaging, comments about her job the first time they'd met and his attitude fanned Anna's irritation.

'Surprising though it may seem, modelling can be a de-manding profession and I take my work seriously. I was paid to do a job in South Africa, not enjoy a freebie holiday,' she informed him coolly.

'Your attitude is commendable,' Damon assured her gravely, although she detected the glimmering amusement in his dark eyes. Nothing infuriated her more than the belief that pretty women were, by definition, airheads. For a second she was tempted to tell him that she had recently completed a four-year home study course and been awarded a business degree, but then thought better of it. Why did it matter what Damon Kouvaris thought of her? she thought defensively. It wasn't as if she cared about his opinion of her.

She returned her attention to her starter and found that her appetite had deserted her. He, on the other hand, was eating with evident enjoyment. She was aware of every movement he made and when he reached for his drink she stared, trans-fixed, as his strong, tanned fingers curled around the stem of the glass.

From her brief conversation with him on Zathos, she

knew that his father had once insisted he should learn every aspect of the building trade. His family might own the multimillion-pound Kouvaris Construction company but Damon had started his working life as a labourer.

Twenty years on, he had an expert knowledge of his trade and, although he now spent most of his time in the boardroom rather than on site, he still retained the superb physique he'd gained through hard physical labour. His hands were strong and darkly tanned. She watched him lift his glass and could not repress a tremor at the thought of those lean fingers caressing her body.

His touch would be slightly abrasive against her skin. She wondered if the black hairs she glimpsed on his wrist covered the whole of his body. Certainly his chest, she decided. She doubted that he shaved his body hair, as was common with many of her male friends in the modelling industry. And his golden tan was from the hot, Greek sun, not hours stretched out on a sunbed.

In the superficial world she inhabited, Damon's overwhelming masculinity was alien and unnerving, but undeniably sexy. He evoked thoughts and feelings within her that were as unexpected as they were shocking. Her tension returned with a vengeance and as her throat closed up she choked on a prawn.

'Easy…try to drink a little water.' His quiet concern made her eyes sting with stupid tears and she forced herself to take a sip of ice-cold water from the glass he held to her lips. 'Better?' His eyes were not black, as she had first thought, but a deep, dark mahogany, velvet soft as he focused intently on her.

'Yes, thank you,' she mumbled, groping for her self-possession to disguise the fact that she felt a fool. Get a grip, she ordered herself impatiently. She spent a good part of her life attending social functions in the company of some of the world's most eligible men. Surely it wasn't beyond her to cope with Damon Kouvaris for a couple of hours without making a complete idiot of herself?

The main course was served but Anna could not do justice to Mrs Jessop's excellent cooking and toyed with her food, hoping to give the appearance that she was eating.

'Are you simply not hungry, or are you one of those women who religiously count every calorie?' Damon murmured in her ear. 'You have a spectacular figure, Anna, but I wouldn't like to see you any thinner,' he added, plainly unperturbed by her fierce glare.

His words were the last straw. How *dared* he make personal comments? She wouldn't be affording him the opportunity to *see* her at all, whatever her shape, Anna vowed furiously, unaware that he could read the murderous thoughts that darkened her eyes to the colour of cobalt.

Anna Christiansen was as exquisite as a fine porcelain figurine, Damon thought appreciatively, unable to tear his gaze from the delicate beauty of her face. Her classically sculpted features were perfect, the tilt of her wide mouth offering a sensual invitation he longed to accept.

It was impossible to travel anywhere in the world without seeing her face on a billboard or featured in a glossy magazine. He'd read somewhere that the cosmetic house she represented had offered her a new contract worth several million pounds and it was easy to see why. With her pale blonde hair drawn back into a sleek chignon and her huge eyes defined by carefully applied make-up, she was every woman's style-icon and every red-blooded male's fantasy.

As his gaze dropped to the soft curve of her mouth he felt his body's involuntary reaction to the sight of her scarlet lips, glistening and moist and so damn sexy that heat surged through him.

He'd wanted her since the moment he'd first seen her on Zathos, but his godson's christening had hardly been the place to indulge his carnal desires. Anna had obviously thought so, too. She had treated him with a cool indifference that had both amused and intrigued him, particularly when her prim air had been unable to disguise her fierce awareness of him.

He'd noted with interest the way her cheeks suffused with colour whenever he approached her. Doubtless it was all part of a clever act, but the innocence of her rosy blush added to her sensual allure and he'd had to forcibly restrain himself from taking her in his arms and exploring her tantalisingly soft, full lips with his own.

He had received the phone call requesting his urgent presence at one of the Kouvaris developments with uncharacteristic regret. For as long as he could remember, work had been his overriding mistress, coming a close second to his family. But for once he'd felt frustrated that he could not spend longer on Zathos to woo the elegant, slender-limbed blonde who dominated his thoughts.

He'd spent much of the last two months in Athens attending to the necessary task of rearranging his personal life, and in particular ending the affair with his mistress. He wanted no messy loose ends to mar his pursuit of Anna and had viewed Filia's tears with irritation. It was not as if Filia had been in love with *him,* but rather his wallet, he acknowledged cynically.

He'd made it clear from the start, as he always did, that he wasn't looking for love and commitment, and could offer neither. Filia had eventually been consoled by several expensive gifts and now he was free and eager to discover if the chemistry he'd felt between him and Anna on Zathos would live up to its explosive promise.

Anna was speaking to him and with an effort he dragged

his mind from the erotic fantasy of exploring her slim body. He guessed from her clipped tone that he had riled her and his lips twitched at the flash of fire in her eyes.

'I fail to see that my eating habits are any of your business, but, if you must know, I have a normal, healthy diet,' she told him indignantly.

'I'm glad to hear it. In that case you'll be able to have dinner with me tomorrow night. I'll pick you up at seven.'

Another guest caught his attention and he smiled as he responded to the query about where exactly in Athens he was based. Beside him Anna seethed silently, waiting for the opportunity to tell him that she was unavailable tomorrow night, or any other night for the foreseeable future.

How dared he just assume that she would jump at his invitation? To her over-sensitive mind it seemed to be another example of his belief that she was a dumb blonde who couldn't think for herself. He was the most arrogant man she had ever met and as soon as she could get a word in edgeways she would turn him down flat.

To her chagrin Damon paid her scant attention for the remainder of the meal and she had drained the last of her coffee and was debating whether Kezia would be offended if she pleaded a headache and went home when he turned to her again.

'Is there anywhere in particular you'd like to go tomorrow night?' he queried casually, as if they had been dating for months. Anna gave him one of her cool smiles guaranteed to freeze the most ardent admirer and swallowed her desire to tell him exactly where she'd like him to go.

'I'm afraid I must turn down your kind offer, tempting though it is,' she said with barely concealed sarcasm. 'I'm busy tomorrow night.'

'That's not a problem,' he assured her blandly. 'We'll make it the following evening.'

'I'm busy then, too.'

'And the next night?' His brows lifted, his tone faintly sardonic now, as if he was growing bored of the game that she was playing.

'I'm afraid not.'

'I had no idea that modelling made such demands on your time.'

'I didn't say I was working,' she snapped, feeling thoroughly hot and flustered. Was his ego so inflated that he couldn't take a simple no for an answer? 'Had it not occurred to you that I could be dating someone else at the moment?'

He paused and reflected for a moment. 'Are you?'

Anna was aware that conversation around the table had lulled and they were attracting attention, Kezia's in particular. It was tempting to lie to him, but innate honesty made her shake her head. 'No,' she admitted ungraciously, her tone sharp. She knew she was overreacting, but she had never felt so acutely aware of a man in her life and she was terrified that he would realise the effect he was having on her.

'So what *are* you doing every evening this week?' Damon enquired silkily, although she wasn't fooled by his indolent tone when she caught the glint of battle in his eyes.

Damn him. How had he managed to turn the conversation around so that she felt guilty for declining what was, in all honesty, a simple request to join him for dinner? She had no reason to feel guilty, she assured herself. If he was conceited enough to believe she was his for the taking, like a ripe plum ready to fall into his hands, he deserved to be disappointed.

'I'm washing my hair,' she snapped, not bothering to disguise the asperity in her tone. She glared at him, quivering with tension as she waited for his response.

'You obviously lead a full life,' he murmured lazily, his mouth curving into a smile that made no effort to hide his amusement. He turned away from her to speak to the guest on the other side of him, leaving Anna with the distinct impression that she had lost the first round.

She was aware of the faintly embarrassed, pitying glances from around the table and knew that her cheeks were scarlet. She'd got what she wanted, hadn't she? Damon could not have made it plainer that he had lost interest in her and the idea of taking her to dinner. So why did she feel so put out?

She didn't want to have dinner with him, she reminded herself irritably, but the words sounded as unconvincing to her own ears as they did when Kezia demanded an explanation later in the evening.

'I thought you liked Damon,' her friend muttered, after insisting that Anna accompany her upstairs to check on Theo. 'He only asked you out to dinner, Anna; it's not as if he issued an invitation to leap into bed with him.'

'I had the impression that one was merely a prelude to the other,' Anna replied dryly. 'You said yourself that Damon Kouvaris is a notorious womaniser and I have no intention of becoming another notch on his bedpost.'

'More's the pity,' Kezia muttered beneath her breath, but Anna's keen ears caught the comment and her eyes narrowed.

'Meaning what, exactly?'

'Meaning that you cannot spend your whole life pushing people away through fear.'

'I'm not afraid of Damon,' Anna replied fiercely, although not entirely truthfully. The enigmatic Greek disturbed her more than she cared to admit.

Kezia glanced at Anna's tense expression and sighed. 'When will you accept that the sins of your father won't necessarily be repeated by every man you meet? Not every man out there is a serial adulterer.'

'Are you honestly suggesting that Damon would be a

committed and faithful lover?' Anna queried tightly. 'His track record is appalling. I know his type, Kezia. I meet men like him every day and, trust me, he's only interested in one thing.'

'Well, he's not getting it from me,' she hissed. She followed Kezia out of the nursery, her steps slowing when a figure emerged from the shadows.

'Damon! You startled us,' Kezia murmured while Anna prayed that a hole would appear beneath her feet.

'Forgive me—Nik said you were checking on Theo and I was wondering if I could take a peep at my godson. I hope I didn't disturb you,' he replied, his smile encompassing them both but his gaze fixed firmly on Anna.

'Not at all, we were just…chatting,' she mumbled, her face flaming at the sardonic expression in his eyes.

'So I heard.' Damon's tone was bland but his smile did not reach his eyes. Anna had been prickly and defensive all evening. He'd assumed she was playing the well-known game of hard to get and he had even been prepared to go along with it for a while. Often, the thrill of the chase proved to be the most enjoyable part of a relationship, he acknowledged cynically.

But the snatches of conversation he had overheard between Anna and Kezia threw a different light on her attitude. The media had exaggerated his reputation as a playboy, but he had never professed to be a saint, he admitted ruefully.

He knew nothing of Anna's family situation, but if her father really had been a serial adulterer then perhaps it explained her unwillingness to acknowledge the attraction that had first flared between them on Zathos. The attraction was, however, undeniably still there; if he'd had any doubts before, he had none now, having noted how she had been unable to keep her eyes off him throughout dinner.

CHAPTER TWO

'IT's been a wonderful evening, Kezia, but I really must go home,' Anna announced firmly when she followed her friend down the sweeping staircase leading from the nursery. Call her a coward, but she doubted her ability to cope with Damon Kouvaris's unsettling presence for a minute longer. 'I've a busy couple of days ahead,' she murmured by way of excuse.

Damon was waiting at the bottom of the stairs. His brows rose quizzically at her words. 'Yes, all that hair-washing must be exhausting,' he commented dulcetly.

Kezia valiantly hid her smile at Anna's furious expression. 'Of course I don't mind. I'll just fetch your jacket,' she choked as she disappeared into the cloakroom, leaving Anna alone with Damon.

The silence stretched between them until Anna was sure he must be able to hear the erratic thud of her heart. She searched her mind for something to say. She spent her life making witty small talk but it seemed that her brain had decamped and all she could think of were stupid inanities that would probably reinforce his belief that she was a brainless blonde.

'So, you're going to be tied up all week? A punishing schedule in the beauty salon, no doubt,' he drawled, his laconic comment inciting her instant wrath.

'Actually I shall be training all week,' she told him stiffly, wishing that the sight of him in his black dinner suit didn't affect her so strongly. She felt as gauche as a teenager and was aware that her voice sounded breathless and girly when she wanted to impress him with the fact that she was a so-phisticated woman of the world.

'Training for what?' Damon couldn't disguise his scepti-cism.

'I'm running a half-marathon around Hyde Park next weekend. The event is to raise money for a number of charities and I'm supporting a charity that is trying to raise funds for a children's hospice. Perhaps you'd like to sponsor me?' she added, lowering her guard slightly. He was reputed to be a multimillionaire and the charity needed all the support it could get. This wasn't the time for pride.

'I'd be delighted. How many miles are you planning to run?'

'Thirteen,' she admitted, her hesitant tone betraying her doubts. Her training schedule hadn't gone quite to plan and it had come as a shock to realise that the race was only a week away. She had a naturally slender, athletic build and worked out in the gym regularly, but thirteen miles suddenly seemed an awfully long way.

'So how far do you run on your training sessions?'

'About half that distance,' she mumbled, 'give or take the odd mile.'

'Ah.' There was a wealth of amusement in his dark eyes. He plainly didn't think she could do it and his scepticism brought her chin up defiantly. She'd show him.

'I'm pretty fit and I don't anticipate any problems,' she told him coolly, crossing her fingers behind her back as she spoke.

Damon stared at her speculatively for a few moments. 'Nik is a devoted father and I imagine he's pledged a large donation in support of the children's charity. I'll match his offer.'

'Are you sure…? I mean, it's a six-figure sum,' she argued faintly.

'Are you saying you don't think the charity could make use of the money?'

'Of course it could.' It might even mean that the children's hospice could open earlier than planned, she acknowledged as she worried her bottom lip with her teeth. 'But are you sure you would be prepared to sponsor me for such a huge amount?' There had to be a catch. She didn't believe for a minute that he would make such a generous offer, even if he hadn't initially realized how much Nik's donation was, without demanding something in return.

She felt his dark gaze skim over her, hovering on the delicate swell of her breasts before sliding lower to her narrow hips and long, slender legs encased in sheer black stockings. The heat in his gaze made her quiver with a mixture of outrage and undeniable awareness. If he dared to make the vile suggestion that she sleep with him in return for sponsoring her, she would be out of the front door before he could blink, having first told him precisely where he could stick his donation.

'I'm in the fortunate position to be able to donate to many charities,' he told her. 'But, tell me, why do you support this particular cause?'

Anna shrugged and tore her gaze from his face. 'It's heartbreaking to think of children's lives blighted by illness. I used to visit Kezia while she was undergoing chemotherapy,' she added. 'She was so brave, as all the sick children I've met since are. If I can use my—' she broke off and laughed deprecatingly '—celebrity status to raise money for the charity, then I'm prepared to do anything.'

Well, almost anything, she amended silently when he

moved closer and lifted his hand to smooth a stray tendril of hair back from her face. It was a curiously intimate gesture and she stiffened, her breath catching in her throat as she inhaled his seductive male scent.

'So, I'll make a significant donation to your good cause and in return you'll run thirteen miles—and…' His sudden smile took her breath away and she found that she was unable to drag her gaze from the sensual curve of his mouth.

'And I'll what?' she demanded suspiciously. She'd known there had to be a catch.

'And you'll agree to have dinner with me,' he completed blandly, the gleam in his eyes telling her that he could read her mind and was aware of her misgivings. 'What are you afraid of, Anna? I promise I don't slurp my soup,' he assured her gravely.

He was openly teasing her and she felt her cheeks burn with a mixture of embarrassment and, God forbid, disappointment. She should feel relieved that he hadn't demanded the right to assuage the desire she had glimpsed in his eyes. Instead she felt thoroughly disconcerted. Maybe she'd read the signs wrong. Perhaps she had been so intent on fighting her awareness of him that she had been mistaken in her belief that the attraction was mutual?

He made the most of her hesitation to slide his hand beneath her chin, tilting her face to his so that she had no option but to meet his gaze. 'Do we have a deal?'

'I suppose so,' she muttered, blushing once more when he grimaced.

'And so graciously accepted,' he drawled, 'it should be an evening to remember.'

Anna resisted the urge to slap him and jerked out of his hold. His arrogance was infuriating and she longed to dent his pride. 'I've just remembered that I don't have a free evening for weeks,' she informed him sweetly.

'That's a pity, because no dinner means no donation,' Damon replied hardly, seemingly unperturbed by the flash of fury in her blue eyes.

'Are you saying that, even if I complete the race, you'll only give your donation after I've had dinner with you?' she queried heatedly, needing to have him spell it out. 'That's blackmail!'

'That's the deal,' he stated with ominous finality. 'Don't look so downhearted, *pedhaki mou*. Who knows? You might even enjoy it.'

'I wouldn't count on it.' She bit back the rest of her angry words and took a hasty step away from him when Kezia returned from the cloakroom, holding her jacket.

'Sorry I was so long,' Kezia murmured, her gaze swinging from Anna's mutinous face to Damon's closed expression.

Anna gave her friend a tight-lipped smile. 'Lovely dinner—will you pass on my compliments to Mrs Jessop, and say good night to Nik for me,' she said briskly.

'Be careful. I wish you weren't driving down those dark country lanes on your own,' Kezia replied concernedly, her frown clearing when Damon waved his car keys in the air.

'Don't worry, I'll be following close behind and I'll see that Anna reaches home safely,' he promised. 'I need to put in a couple of hours work tonight, before a meeting tomorrow morning,' he explained apologetically. 'Many thanks for a delightful evening, Kezia.'

'But I thought…' Anna glared at him, incensed by his faintly proprietorial air. She didn't need a bodyguard, for heaven's sake. 'I assumed you were staying here, at Otterbourne,' she muttered as she followed him down the front steps of the house.

'No, it's easier for me to be based in central London. And besides, Nik and Kezia are so wrapped up in each other that I feel like a cuckoo in the love nest,' he added with a grin that caused her insides to melt.

'Well, I hope you're not cutting your evening short because of some misguided belief that you need to escort me home,' she said crisply as she unlocked her low-slung sports car and slid behind the wheel. 'I'm perfectly capable of taking care of myself.'

'I'm sure you are, *pedhaki mou.*' The sudden sultriness of his tone caught her attention and her irritation increased when she discovered that his gaze was focused intently on the way her skirt had ridden up, exposing a length of slender thigh. 'Drive carefully, Anna. I'll be in touch,' he added mockingly, causing her to slam the door so forcefully that the car shook.

'Terrific,' she muttered beneath her breath. She could hardly wait. She swung out of the drive, her mood as black as the pitch-dark lanes, and her temper was not improved by the gleam of his headlights following at a safe distance behind her. It was yet another example of Damon's arrogance, she brooded. She had taken care of herself for most of her life and she valued her independence. She didn't need an overbearing, damnably sexy Greek to suddenly muscle in.

Once on the motorway she pressed her foot down on the accelerator and felt the familiar thrill of pleasure as the car surged forwards. Her top-of-the-range, bright red sports car was an extravagance, especially when she spent most of her time driving around town, where it drank petrol. But here on the open road she could indulge her passion for speed and with luck lose her would-be protector.

Goodbye, Damon! With a satisfied smile she selected a CD and turned up the volume. She flew along in the fast lane and reached her junction in record time, slowing as she turned onto the slip-road leading from the motorway before stopping at the red light. A car pulled up in the next lane and when she turned her head her smile faded. Damn him! He must have been right behind her the whole way, she realised, glaring at him when he gave a mocking salute.

Even from this distance she was aware of the challenging gleam in his eyes and as their gazes clashed she found it impossible to turn away. It was dark but she could make out his profile—the sharp angle of his cheekbones and that square chin that hinted at a stubborn determination.

The only softness about his appearance was the way his thick hair curled onto his collar. He was the most gorgeous, sensual man she had ever met, she conceded, her reverie rudely shattered by an impatient hooting from behind that warned her the lights had changed to green. Thoroughly flummoxed and hot cheeked, she crunched the gears before finally pulling away.

He really was the bitter end, she thought irritably some ten minutes later when she turned into the parking area outside her flat and he drew up beside her. What was he waiting for now—a medal, or an invitation up to her flat for coffee? He was out of luck on both counts but innate good manners made her walk over to his car.

'Thanks for seeing me back,' she murmured politely.

'No problem. I'll wait until you're safely inside.'

She was often fearful of who could be lurking in the bushes on either side of the communal front door and hated the short trip across the car park in the dark, but Damon's tone irritated her. 'I'm a big girl now and I really can look after myself, you know,' she drawled.

'I'm not convinced, *pedhaki mou*. For one thing, you drive too fast,' he replied bluntly, the note of censure in his tone causing her hackles to rise.

'I'm an excellent driver,' she snapped indignantly. 'I might drive fast, but I'm always careful.'

He surveyed her silently with his dark, brooding gaze. His eyes were hooded, giving no clue to his thoughts, but somehow he made her feel about six years old.

'So, occasionally I like to live dangerously,' she bit out

belligerently, placing her hands on her hips in a gesture of silent challenge.

His low chuckle caused her to grind her teeth in irritation. 'Then I can only hope that our dinner date is one of those occasions. Now off you go, before I decide to escort you up to your flat,' he warned softly, ignoring her indignant gasp. 'Good night, Anna, and sweet dreams.'

The sound of his mocking laughter followed her across the car park, but Anna refused to award him another glance and marched up the front steps, her back ramrod-straight. Damon Kouvaris was the devil incarnate, but if he thought she would allow him to disturb her calm, well-ordered life, he'd better think again.

Unfortunately the memory of Damon's ruggedly handsome face disturbed her dreams to the extent that she woke the following morning feeling as though she had barely slept at all. Ahead of her lay a week of serious training for the half-marathon, but the thought of spending the day at the local sports centre, pounding the running track, held little appeal and with a groan she burrowed beneath the duvet.

It was late morning before she arrived at the track, spurred on by the knowledge that she had promised the children's charity her support and couldn't let them down. Even discounting Damon's incredible sponsorship offer, she was set to raise many thousands of pounds for the charity. The event was to be televised, with many celebrities taking part, all hoping to raise public awareness, as well as funds for their chosen cause. Pride dictated that she didn't make a complete fool of herself in front the cameras, and, although she hated to admit it—in front of Damon.

An hour later her pride was distinctly shaky, as were her legs. The early June sunshine was surprisingly warm and she was hot and breathless as she strove to keep her pace. The other runners on the track had all lapped her effortlessly and she sighed at the sound of footsteps behind her. How did they make it look so easy? she wondered despairingly.

'How's the training going? Have you run thirteen miles yet?' The familiar honeyed tones caused her to miss her footing and she stumbled and would have tripped if a strong hand hadn't quickly reached out to save her.

'What are *you* doing here?' she demanded crossly, irritated at the way her body was reacting with humiliating eagerness to the sight of Damon. Last night he had looked stunning in a formal dinner suit but today, in running shorts and black vest-top, he was spectacular.

Her eyes made a fleeting inspection of his broad shoulders and impressive, muscle-bound chest before sliding lower, over his shorts before coming to rest on his powerful thighs and long, tanned legs. His athletic build and superb muscle definition caused a peculiar weakness in the pit of her stomach. Cramp, she told herself irritably as she tore her eyes from his brooding gaze and stared along the track. 'How did you know I was here?'

'You told me last night that you intended to put in some training this week, and when I called at your flat your neighbour informed me that she'd seen you leave, carrying a kit bag. It didn't take much to work out that you were probably at the nearest sports centre,' he answered dryly, his eyes raking over her so that Anna felt acutely conscious that she must look a mess. She could feel the beads of sweat that had formed above her top lip and tried to capture them with the tip of her tongue, hoping to hide the evidence that she was exhausted.

'Quite the Sherlock Holmes, aren't you?' she snapped sarcastically, watching the way his eyes narrowed as they focused on the frantic movements of her tongue. 'Well, now that you've found me, what do you want? You're interrupting my training.'

'Do all forms of physical exercise make you so grumpy?' he queried with a grin, seemingly unconcerned by her unfriendly attitude. 'I do hope not,' he added dulcetly, his eyes glinting with amusement at her furious glare. 'You look tired, *pedhaki mou*. I think you should take a break.'

'I'm fine for several more laps yet,' she lied. She shook her thick plait over her shoulder and started to jog once more. 'Why have you decided to appoint yourself as my nanny?'

'Oh, I have my reasons,' he murmured, keeping pace beside her with infuriating ease. She felt his gaze trawl over her crop-top and the smooth expanse of her flat stomach before sliding lower to her tight, Lycra running shorts that clung to her hips and moulded her neat bottom. 'Although I prefer to think of myself as your personal trainer.'

'I don't need a trainer. I need you to leave me alone.' Her voice came out as a wail of frustration and she swung her head round to stare at him, thought better of it and kept on running. 'Look, Damon, you've already blackmailed me into having dinner with you. Let's just leave it at that,' she muttered breathlessly. 'I don't want to see you, I don't want to spend time with you, and I don't date.'

'You don't date. *Theos!* Hardly a week goes by without a photo of you and your latest celebrity boyfriend posing for the tabloids,' he retorted sardonically, unable to disguise his impatience. 'Reports of your love life fill more newspaper columns than any political intrigue. What's the real issue here, Anna? Is it the fact that I'm not some suitably famous TV soap star? I can assure you, I'm more of a man than any of the pretty boys you seem to favour.'

'Oh, for heaven's sake.' She halted in the middle of the track and glared at him in impotent fury. His arrogance would be funny if she hadn't recognised the intrinsic truth of his last statement. Damon's flagrant, raw masculinity unsettled her more than any other man she'd met.

Nothing would induce her to reveal that her alleged lovers were simply friends who for their own reasons found it useful to act the role of her escort. Living in the media spotlight was akin to living in a goldfish bowl and over the years she had learned to dismiss most of the rubbish that was written about her and her so-called wild love life. Now, as she stared at Damon she felt sickened by the hint of contempt in his eyes.

'How dare you turn up here and…harass me?' she exploded. 'I'm not some blonde bimbo and, despite what you might have read in the tabloids, I am not an easy lay.'

She was shocked by the force of her emotions, the feeling of hurt, and blinked hard to dispel the stupid tears that had gathered in her eyes. She rarely cried, and never over a man. Years of witnessing her mother's disastrous love life and subsequent slide into depression had taught her they weren't worth it.

After her parents' bitter divorce she had vowed never to be emotionally or financially dependent on anyone. The Ice Princess had a heart of glass and she felt a shaft of genuine fear that Damon seemed to possess the power to shatter it.

'Did you really think you could just click your fingers and I would be yours for the taking?' she demanded stiffly. 'Because if so, I've got news for you.'

'Credit me with a little more finesse, Anna,' he replied lazily. 'But I can't deny I hoped for the chance to explore the awareness between us that we both recognised on Zathos. And why not?' he continued. 'We're both consenting adults. Why shouldn't we indulge in a mutually enjoyable affair?'

'You mean sex without the inconvenience of messy emotions?' she said scathingly, ignoring the devil in her head that was asking the question—why not? At least Damon was being honest. He wasn't trying to woo her with meaningless romantic gestures and promises that they both knew he wouldn't keep. Why not follow the dictates of her body for once rather than listen to the cool voice of common sense?

She sensed instinctively that Damon would be a passionate yet sensitive lover. But he would also be her first. It would almost be worth it, just to see the shock on his face when he realised she was a virgin, she brooded darkly. It was obvious that he believed every piece of tittle-tattle written about her and assumed that she led an active and varied sex life. She could imagine his disappointment when he discovered her inexperience.

Would he offer to tutor her? she wondered, heat coursing through her veins at the mental image of his hands gliding over her body, teaching her the language of love.

Stifling a gasp, she tore her gaze from his darkly handsome face. His heavy brows were drawn into a frown, his eyes hooded, hiding his thoughts, but she was aware of the electricity between them—an invisible force that set her nerve endings on fire and increased her acute consciousness of every breath he took.

What was she thinking of? She must be mad to have considered even for a second, becoming involved with him. In Damon Kouvaris she saw her father—handsome, charismatic and unable to remain faithful to one woman for more than five minutes. She would not repeat the mistakes her mother had made, she assured herself fiercely and she tilted her chin and stared at him coolly.

'I'm sorry to disappoint you but I have no intention of indulging in any kind of a relationship with you, certainly not a casual fling while you happen to be in London. You must be mistaken about Zathos,' she added airily. 'I don't remember there being anything between us. In fact I'd practically forgotten you.'

'Is that so?' Beneath his indolent, faintly amused tone, she detected anger and steeled herself to fight him off when he caught hold of her shoulder and spun her round to face him. His dark eyes were mesmerising and she found herself trapped by the sensual heat of his gaze as he slowly lowered his head.

He was going to kiss her. Her brain sent out an urgent warning telling her to jerk free of his grasp, but she was boneless, enveloped in a haze of quivering anticipation as she waited for his lips to claim hers.

She had wanted this since she had first met him on Zathos, she admitted silently, unwittingly parting her lips in readiness. She needed him to take control, to tear down her defences and capture her mouth in a hungry, elemental kiss that would ignore her token resistance. Time seemed to be suspended as she waited, her eyes closed against the glare of the sun. She could feel his warm breath fan her cheek and as her desperation increased she swayed towards him, her senses leaping when she inhaled his clean, seductive scent.

'In that case I suppose I'll just have to content myself with overseeing your training.' His calm, matter-of-fact voice shattered the spell he had cast over her and her eyes flew open to clash with his glinting gaze. Colour scalded her cheeks and she felt sick with humiliation when he released her and stepped away, his bland smile telling her he was aware of her disappointment. She had offered herself up like…like a sacrificial virgin, she acknowledged furiously, and he had rejected her.

'I don't need any help. I prefer to train on my own,' she muttered, her voice thick with mortification. Spinning round on her heels, she set off at a pace that was impossible to maintain. She was going too fast, too soon, her coach would have advised her, but right now all she could think of was putting some space between her and the most infuriating man she had ever met. 'Just go away, Damon, and leave me alone,' she flung over her shoulder.

Damon watched her disappear along the track and felt the familiar ache in his groin as he admired her impossibly long, tanned legs and the tantalising sway of her *derrière*. If only it were that easy to let her go, he thought grimly.

He'd been intrigued from the first—drawn not just by her beauty, but by the woman herself. At first glance Anneliese Christiansen appeared every inch the glamorous, sophisticated supermodel who featured regularly in the gossip columns. But he was beginning to realise that the real Anna was a far more complex mixture of emotions.

For a start she was not as worldly as he had expected. She reminded him of a young colt, skittish and nervy, and ready to back away the minute he came near. Persuading her into his bed was not going to be as easy as he had first assumed. It would take time and patience to win her trust and he had a short supply of both.

Common sense told him to walk away. The world was full of stunning blondes and he preferred women who required little emotional maintenance. But for the past two months Anna had filled his mind to the exclusion of almost everything else, even business.

It was a new experience for him and one that he didn't enjoy, which was why he had decided to make use of his time in England to take his desire for her to its logical conclusion. He hadn't anticipated such a robust rebuttal, he acknowledged wryly, but Anna's determination to ignore the chemistry between them only served to further his interest.

He wanted her. And whatever Damon Kouvaris wanted, he invariably got.

CHAPTER THREE

ANNA kept on running until her heart felt as though it would burst. Even then she pushed herself on, lap after lap, and every time she completed a circuit she glanced hopefully over to where she had left her kit bag by the side of the track, praying that Damon would have gone.

He was still there, sprawled on the grass, the sun gilding his bronzed shoulders and strong, muscular thighs revealed below the hem of his running shorts. Not that he had done much running, she noted irritably. He had simply sat there, sunning himself—a demigod in designer shades, watching her run until she was near to the point of collapse.

With a muttered oath she slowed her steps and headed across the track. If his presence as spectator was a battle of wills, she was ready to admit defeat. Her legs felt like jelly— a fact that had nothing to do with the sight of him, she assured herself when she reached the spot where she had dumped her bag.

Affecting an air of supreme uninterest, she ignored him and reached into her bag for her water bottle. The few mouthfuls of liquid remaining in the bottle did nothing to quench her thirst but the thought of walking back to the sports complex to refill it was beyond her and she sank to the ground, burying her face in the sweet-smelling grass.

'If you intend to run at that pace for the whole race, you'll never make it past the halfway mark,' Damon commented idly.

'Go to hell.' The fact that he was right did nothing to improve her temper and she turned her head to glare at him, further incensed as she watched him drink from his own water canister. There was something innately earthy and sensual about the way he gulped thirstily and her eyes focused on the convulsive movement of his throat when he swallowed.

'Here.' He must have felt her eyes on him and handed her the canister. Desperation overcame pride and she sat up and took it from him, put it to her lips and drank. 'You should bring more water with you; one small bottle isn't enough in this heat. Although it defies common sense to train during the hottest part of the day anyway,' he added, as if he were speaking to a small child.

'Anything else?' she drawled sarcastically. She lay back in the grass and allowed her eyes to drift shut. He was the most arrogant, overbearing man she had ever met and she wanted to tell him to get lost, but she was too exhausted to speak, and, anyway, she doubted he would listen.

The running track was set far back from the road and all she could hear was the piercingly sweet song of a skylark hovering high above. It was the sound of summer, she thought sleepily, turning her face to the sun, but as a shadow fell across her she opened her eyes again to find Damon leaning over her.

'You shouldn't lie out in the full glare of the sun without protection. I'm just making sure you don't burn,' he added equably when she frowned at the close proximity of his body next to hers.

He was lying on his side, propped up on one elbow so that his upper body shielded her from the sun. He had removed his sunglasses so that she could see the fine lines around his eyes, although his thoughts were concealed behind impossibly long black lashes. A lock of hair had fallen forwards onto his brow and she resisted the urge to reach up and run her fingers through the gleaming black silk.

He was too much, and right now she was too tired to do battle with him, she conceded weakly, dragging her eyes from the sight of his broad chest, barely covered by his black sleeveless sports vest. He must spend hours in the gym developing those biceps, she thought derisively, but somehow she couldn't imagine him wasting his time lifting weights.

'What kind of sport do you enjoy?' she queried, blushing furiously at the wicked glint in his eyes. There was no doubting the form of physical exercise he liked best.

'I like to play squash. I find it more challenging than tennis. Other than that I enjoy swimming in the pool at my villa back home, and when I was younger I belonged to a boxing club and was junior national champion for three years running,' he told her on a note of quiet pride.

'You enjoyed fighting?' Anna wrinkled her nose. 'I hate that kind of aggressive, contact sport.'

'Actually boxing requires extreme discipline and mental agility, not just brute strength,' he said with a smile. 'It's an excellent way for boys and young men to release the build-up of testosterone.'

'I imagine you had more than your fair share of that,' she muttered dryly. Even at an early age he must have attracted female attention like bees to honey. She could picture him as a swaggering, cocky youth, hell-bent on having his own way. 'You must have driven your parents to distraction.'

'Probably,' he agreed cheerfully, 'but my father curbed my excesses by sending me to work on building projects. I may have been the heir to a multimillion-pound fortune but he believed that I should start at the bottom and earn my place in Kouvaris Construction. He taught me a lot,' he added softly and Kezia caught the note of affection and respect in his voice.

'I'm sure your parents are very proud of you,' she said, recalling a recent newspaper article detailing the astounding success of the Kouvaris Construction group under his directorship. 'Where are they now—do they live near you in Greece?'

'Sadly they've both passed away. My father died ten years ago and my mother followed soon after. He was her reason for living and she simply couldn't bear to be without him,' he added quietly.

'I'm sorry.' She sat up, feeling suddenly restless. Maybe it was the talk about happy families, she thought bleakly. Damon had spoken with such conviction of the love his parents had shared for each other, but she found it unsettling.

She would never award a man so much power over her that he became her reason for living, she vowed fiercely. She had witnessed firsthand the damage such strong emotions could wreak. Her father had been the centre of her mother's universe and his infidelities had almost destroyed her.

'So, do you have any other family—brothers and sisters?' she asked as curiosity won over her initial wariness of him.

'One sister, Catalina.' He rolled onto his back and tucked his arms behind his head so that Anna's eyes were drawn unwittingly to the way his vest top had ridden up, revealing a sprinkling of black hairs that arrowed down over his taut stomach.

'She was only eighteen when my parents died and we're very close. In fact we share a villa just outside Athens. Fortunately a very large villa, which is divided into two separate homes now that Catalina is married and has her own family,' he added with a laugh. 'We frequently all meet up for meals in the communal courtyard, but I admit I like my own space.'

He paused, as if he was about to say something else, and Anna waited expectantly, but then he shook his head. 'That's enough about me. Now it's your turn.' He stretched out a hand and caught hold of her long, pale gold plait. 'I assume from your colouring and name that you were born in Scandinavia?'

'No, my father is Swedish but my mother's English and I was born here in London. I used to visit my grandparents in Stockholm when I was a child, but I haven't seen them for a long time,' she explained, adding quietly, 'not since my parents split up. The divorce was acrimonious and caused a huge rift in the family.'

'That's a pity; you must miss them. Are you close to your parents?'

'Not particularly.' She jumped up and busied herself with collecting her water bottle and zipping up her bag. 'I was sent away to boarding-school when I was thirteen and I didn't see them that much.' She gave him a brisk smile, indicating her desire to change the subject.

'You didn't enjoy living away from home, I take it?' he asked softly, studying her closed expression speculatively.

'On the contrary, I loved it. It taught me to be independent and stand on my own two feet. The most valuable lesson I've ever learned is never to rely on anyone else.' She swung her bag over her shoulder and began to walk away from him. 'I have to go now,' she stated bluntly, her tone clearly indicating that she didn't expect him to join her.

It was plain that even the most innocent enquiries about her personal life, and, in particular, her family, were off limits, Damon realised. He jumped to his feet and strolled after her. Beneath her bravado he had detected a note of real pain in her voice when she'd spoken of her parents' divorce.

Thirteen was a notoriously difficult age, particularly for girls, he mused, remembering his sister during her teenage years.

He had been lucky enough to enjoy an idyllic childhood, brought up in a happy and stable environment by parents whose love for each other and their children had never been in doubt. Perhaps Anna's childhood experiences had caused real emotional damage and contributed towards her fiercely defended independence?

From the articles about her in the press, he had imagined her to be shallow and spoilt, exchanging one handsome actor boyfriend for another with startling regularity. Equality between the sexes suited him fine, he acceded, his eyes focusing on her endlessly long, slender legs as she marched on ahead of him. He was happy to admit that he wasn't looking for the commitment of a long-term relationship.

Everything he'd read about Anna confirmed that she was a sophisticated woman of the world and he was impatient to take her to bed. But, meeting her again, he had glimpsed an air of vulnerability about her that was as disturbing as it was unexpected. Beneath her ice-cool beauty there lurked a deep well of emotions and to his astonishment he was aware of a tug of protectiveness of her.

'So, are you an only child?' he queried. 'Or are there other, equally stunning Christiansens waiting to take the modelling world by storm?'

Anna paused fractionally, her impatient glare saying louder than words that her private life was none of his business. 'I have a couple of stepsisters from my father's second marriage, but we're not close.'

She almost choked on the understatement. As a teenager she had hated the fact that her adored father preferred to live with his new wife's children rather than her. Her jealousy had caused friction on her monthly visits to see him and had finally led Lars Christiansen to break off all but the most cursory contact. Her feeling of rejection had been unbearable, but it had been a salutary life lesson, she acknowledged grimly.

'Do you still keep in contact with your father?' Damon asked curiously.

'Christmas cards, the occasional birthday card if he remembers,' she replied shortly. 'He lives in Sweden now and is currently going through his third divorce. My mother has recently married again for the third time, although I can't imagine why. The whole concept of marriage leaves me cold.'

'Perhaps your parents' experiences are the reason why none of your relationships last longer than a few weeks,' Damon mused. 'Your childhood has left you with a fear of commitment. Is that why you flit from one partner to another?'

They had reached the entrance to the sports centre and Anna swung round, almost incandescent with fury. She balanced on the top step, her eyes glinting with temper. Once again his blithe assumption that the tabloid reports concerning her love life were true hurt more that it should. Why should she give a damn what he thought? And why should she listen to his amateur psychobabble about the effects of her childhood?

'You're hardly one to talk about commitment, Damon,' she snapped scathingly. 'Your reputation as a playboy is well documented—a multimillionaire womaniser with the morals of an alley cat, or so I've heard,' she added, ignoring the flash of anger in his dark eyes. 'Rumour has it that you take what you want and who you want with a ruthless disregard for other people's emotions, but I warn you now, you're not having me!'

She spun on her heels and marched across the foyer

towards the changing rooms before he had time to reply. Damon's expression of stunned surprise was almost comical—she doubted he had ever been spoken to with such brutal honesty before, but she had never felt less like laughing. He had practically accused her of being a tart, she remembered when she stood beneath the shower and allowed her angry tears to fall.

As one of the world's most photographed women, she had grown used to the constant gossip and speculation that surrounded her private life. It was a side to her job that she loathed and occasionally her legal team would demand a retraction from the press or threaten to sue over a particularly scurrilous article.

But for the most part she had learned to live with the fact that, in the media's eyes, she was public property and she treated their intrusion with an air of cool disdain. Hiding her true feelings had become a matter of pride and she couldn't understand why Damon's opinion, of all people, mattered so much.

After showering, she slipped into slim fitting jeans and white T-shirt, donned a pair of strappy sandals and combed her hair loose so that it could dry naturally. She strolled through the foyer and paused to inspect the day's menu displayed on the blackboard outside the cafeteria despite her awareness of the mountain of paperwork awaiting her at home. Fortunately there was no sight of Damon and as her tension eased she was aware that she was starving.

'Anna, are you going to eat with us today?'

She turned at the sound of the distinctive Italian accent and smiled at Roberto, the manager of the cafeteria. Under his directorship, the cafeteria had developed into an innovative restaurant with an excellent reputation for fresh, beautifully prepared food. In the summer she often ate her lunch outside on the terrace, close to the stream that meandered through the grounds of the sports complex.

'I admit I'm tempted,' she replied, discarding the idea of a sandwich back at her flat in favour of one of Roberto's delicacies.

'I've prepared your favourite—Salade Niçoise,' Roberto informed her with a grin. 'Your friend is already waiting at your usual table.'

'Oh, *is* he.' Her appetite instantly vanished, to be replaced with simmering annoyance, but she liked Roberto and had no option but to follow him out onto the terrace.

Damon was sitting at the table beside the stream. *Her* table, she noted irritably, her smile slipping the moment Roberto had gone. 'Why are you here? I thought I'd made it plain that I didn't want to see you again,' she snapped, mindful of the other guests who were enjoying lunch alfresco.

'You need to eat properly after all that exercise,' Damon replied calmly, seemingly unperturbed by the storm brewing in her navy blue eyes. 'And I don't mean just a snatched sandwich while you're catching up on your paperwork.'

Was the man a mind-reader? She sincerely hoped not, Anna thought darkly as she absorbed the impact of him in cream chinos and a black polo shirt, unfastened at the neck to reveal the tanned column of his throat. He was seriously sexy but she would rather die than give him the satisfaction of knowing how much he affected her.

'I don't want to have lunch with you,' she muttered fiercely, placing her hands on her hips and glaring at him. Damon seemed determined to challenge her and she felt like stamping her foot in temper.

'Are you always so childish?' he queried mildly.

'Are you always so pigheaded?'

They seemed to have reached checkmate, but as she

stood, glowering at him, Roberto appeared, his face beaming as he brought out their lunch.

'You're causing a scene. For your friend's sake why don't you be a good girl and sit down?' Damon instructed, the hint of steel beneath his indolent tone causing her to subside into a chair.

'That wasn't a scene—trust me, I can do much better than that,' she growled warningly before pinning a smile on her face to greet Roberto. 'That looks divine, Roberto—as usual,' she complimented approvingly when the chef set her meal before her.

'Enjoy,' Roberto said happily. 'I see you are training hard for the race. Now you need to eat.' He winked at Damon. 'Anna has the face of an angel, huh? But I tell you, she has a big heart. She's always busy raising money for different charities. Are you going to watch her run the marathon?'

'I wouldn't miss it for the world,' Damon assured the other man, carefully avoiding Anna's poisonous glare. 'I'll be there supporting her the whole way.'

The thought was enough to ruin Anna's appetite but she couldn't leave her meal without hurting Roberto's feelings and so she picked up her fork. Damon ignored her while he concentrated on his own meal and after a few mouthfuls she found herself slowly start to relax. The food was heavenly and she ate with enjoyment, her senses soothed by the gentle trickling sound of the stream.

'Better than a sandwich?' The gentle query brought her head up and she discovered that Damon had finished his meal and was quietly watching her.

'Much, although the paperwork is still waiting,' she admitted with a rueful smile. She was not by nature a sulker and, aided by Roberto's culinary skill, her anger had gradually melted away. 'I hadn't realised how hungry I was,' she said awkwardly. 'Thank you.'

'My pleasure.'

It was amazing how two little words could evoke such a fevered reaction within her, she thought despairingly as heat suffused her whole body. She was so agonisingly aware of Damon that it seemed as if nothing else existed. The voices of the other diners faded and the air seemed so still that she was conscious of every breath he took.

'How long do you plan to stay in England?' she burst out, wincing as her voice sounded over-loud to her ears.

'I'm not entirely sure—it depends on a number of things,' he replied obliquely, his smile causing Anna's heart to thud erratically. She felt an irrational urge to snatch his sunglasses from his face in order to read his thoughts but had to content herself with reaching into her bag for her own shades. It might be cowardly but she felt measurably safer with them on. Damon seemed to have the disturbing knack of reading her mind and she preferred to keep her thoughts to herself.

'How about you? Do you have any plans to travel in the near future?'

'I have assignments in New York coming up but I purposefully kept the next couple of weeks clear. Time to prepare for the charity race and time afterwards to recover from it,' she added with a sudden, disarming grin.

It was her smile that did it for him, Damon acknowledged silently, his eyes focusing on the tilt of her wide mouth. When she smiled her face lit up and she was transformed from classically beautiful to simply breathtaking.

He wondered what she would do if he gave into the urge to lean across the table and claim her lips with his own—and to hell with the other diners. Most women of his acquaintance would giggle and lower their lashes, perhaps wind their arms around his neck to respond to his kiss. Anna would undoubtedly throw the coffee-pot at his head, he accepted with a wry smile as he sought to bring his rampaging hormones under control.

'What led you to choose modelling as a career?' he queried. 'Apart from the obvious, of course.'

'The obvious?' Anna frowned, clearly puzzled.

'Your looks—I'm sure I'm not the first man to tell you that the combination of your features is utterly exquisite.'

The words were uttered with an air of clinical detachment that made Anna shiver. It was true that she received countless compliments—none of which affected her in the slightest. Why then did Damon's cool assessment send a quiver of fierce pleasure through her?

She wanted to say something flippant but her mouth was suddenly dry and she reached for her glass of water with a hand that shook slightly.

'I never made a conscious decision to become a model,' she told him when she could trust herself to speak. 'When I left school, most of my friends, including Kezia, went to university, but I had no clear idea of what I wanted to do with my life. When I was "spotted", walking down the Kings Road, it seemed like a godsend—I'd fallen behind with the rent on my bedsit and had no idea how I was going to pay it.' She shrugged her shoulders expressively. 'To be honest, I thought I'd give modelling a go for a couple of months, until I was back on my feet financially. I never expected it to become a career.'

'Yet your success is astounding,' Damon commented. 'Do you enjoy modelling?'

'I enjoy the money,' she replied bluntly. 'I enjoy the fact that I'm financially independent and don't have to rely on anyone else for anything.'

For anyone else, read any man, Damon guessed. What had happened in her past to make her so mistrustful of relationships? A broken love affair perhaps—or did her wariness stem from events in her childhood? 'Financial security is obviously important to you, but isn't the predicted career-span of even an internationally successful model such as yourself notoriously short?'

'Hopefully I'll continue to work for a few more years and I already have a significant property portfolio, which I plan to extend. The buy-to-let market in London is booming, as I'm sure you know, and I enjoy being a landlord much more than a tenant.'

'So, behind that angelic face lies the brain of a ruthless businesswoman,' Damon teased lightly.

'I know what it's like to be at rock-bottom,' she replied seriously. 'The few months between when I left school and was taken on by the modelling agency were hellish. I had no job, no money and often had to rely on friends for somewhere to stay.'

'But surely you could have lived with one of your parents after you'd left boarding-school?' Damon demanded, unable to disguise his shock. She had been little more than a child and yet it sounded as though her family had abandoned her. No wonder she was so desperate for financial security.

'My father was busy with his new family. We had already grown apart and his wife made it clear that she didn't view a difficult teenager as a welcome addition to the household,' Anna revealed, unable to disguise the hint of bitterness in her voice. 'My mother was married to her second husband by then and...' she hesitated fractionally before admitting quietly '...there were reasons why I had to leave home.'

Something in her voice caught Damon's attention. He wanted to ask what those reasons were but even across the width of the table he could feel her tension.

The sun was shining as brightly as ever but, despite its warmth, Anna shivered. She felt as though a black cloud had settled over her, suffocating her with the disturbing memories she would rather forget. Her stepfather's sly, leering face filled her mind and she felt the familiar feeling of nausea sweep over her when she remembered his hot breath on her skin…his hands touching her at every casual opportunity.

'Anna, are you all right?' Damon's voice seemed to sound from a long way off and she blinked and forced her mind back to the present. He was watching her, his dark brows drawn into a frown of concern.

'I'm fine, just a little tired, that's all,' she quickly reassured him, managing a shaky smile. 'I mustn't keep you. I'm sure you're a busy man, Damon,' she added briskly as she stood up. 'Thank you again for lunch.'

'Where are you parked? I'll see you to your car.' He had already walked round the table to pick up her bag, and before she realised his intention he slid a supporting arm around her waist. 'You look very pale, *pedhaki mou*. I don't think you should drive.'

'I don't intend to. My flat's not far from here and I walked through the park this morning. Damon, I'm perfectly okay,' she said sharply. She was so intent on fighting her reaction to the brush of his thigh against hers that she did not notice that he had led her over to his car.

'Here we are—in you get,' he said cheerfully.

She glared at him when he opened the passenger door. 'I've told you, I'll walk.'

'Do you want to fight about it?' He stood, blocking her path, his arms folded resolutely across his chest in a stance that told her she wasn't going anywhere.

She had lost that sickly pallor, Damon noted with satisfaction. Something had seriously bothered her back there, but now wasn't the time to try and draw the truth from her. Instead he had hoped to focus her mind back on the present by deliberately provoking her temper and, from the hectic

colour staining her cheeks, it appeared that he had suc-
ceeded.

'You are the most infuriating man I have ever met,' she
snapped furiously as she conceded defeat and subsided into
the car. She turned her head when he slid behind the wheel
and pointedly ignored him for the short journey back to her
flat. It was only when he turned into the car park and cut the
engine that she swung back to face him, her eyes wide and
suspiciously bright.

'What do you want from me?' she demanded huskily, the
tremor in her voice causing a peculiar pain in Damon's
stomach. The naked vulnerability in her eyes disturbed him
more than he cared to admit.

'A little of your time, a chance to get to know one another
better and explore what we started on Zathos,' he replied
quietly.

'We didn't start anything.' Her fierce rejection of his
words was instant and laced with panic as she fumbled to
release her seat belt. 'Your imagination must have been
playing tricks on you, Damon. There was nothing.'

'No?' He moved before she had time to react, curving his
hand around her neck to cup her nape before lowering his
head to capture her mouth in a brief, hard kiss.

The moment he touched her Anna tensed, waiting for the
familiar feeling of revulsion to fill her. It didn't come.
Instead of reliving unpleasant memories from the past, her
mind seemed to be a blank canvas where nothing existed
except the warm pleasure of his mouth on hers. His tongue
explored the shape of her lips with delicate precision; an un-
hurried, evocative tasting that caused a trembling to start
deep inside her. To her astonishment she found herself
wanting more, but as she parted her lips he broke the kiss
and drew back to stare into her wide, shell-shocked eyes.

'In my imagination?' he taunted. 'I don't think so, Anna.

The chemistry between us on Zathos was white hot, and it still burns—for both of us. The question is, what are we going to do about it?'

CHAPTER FOUR

ANNA spent the rest of the day scrubbing and polishing her flat, hoping that frenzied activity would prevent her from thinking about Damon. She could no longer deny that she was attracted to him but fear had seen her flee from his car as if the devil himself were in pursuit.

The memory of his kiss lingered, however. She couldn't forget the feel of his mouth on hers, the pleasure his warm, firm lips had evoked, and she was shocked by the realisation that she hadn't wanted him to stop.

She spent the evening ploughing through a mountain of paperwork, but, despite the fact that it was past midnight before she crawled into bed, she slept badly for the second night in succession.

It was Damon's fault, she thought grumpily the next morning, pulling on her trainers and running gear ready for another session at the sports track. He had stormed into her life like a tornado, ripping down her fragile defences and leaving her emotions in tatters.

The doorbell pealed as she was gulping down a second cup of coffee and she opened the door to be presented with an exquisite bouquet of cream roses.

'I was told to give you these,' the delivery boy muttered, handing her two large bottles of spring-water. 'The Greek bloke said I was to be sure to tell you to take them to the track with you.' He shrugged his shoulders indifferently. 'I guess the message means more to you than it does to me.'

Murmuring her thanks, Anna closed the door and carried the flowers back to the kitchen before ripping open the attached envelope with fingers that shook slightly.

'Keep up with the training—I'm looking forward to seeing you cross the finish line,' Damon had written, the sight of his bold signature causing her heart to flip in her chest. His arrogance was insufferable, she thought furiously. For a second she seriously debated stuffing the flowers into the rubbish bin. His note was a subtle reminder that he intended to hold her to her agreement to have dinner with him after the charity race, but to her intense irritation she was unable to repress a little shiver of anticipation at the thought of seeing him again.

The word *no* did not seem to feature in Damon Kouvaris's vocabulary, she decided as she rammed the bottles of water into her kit bag. It was about time someone told him he couldn't always have his own way. But as she inhaled the delicate perfume of the blooms she could not bring herself to destroy them and placed them in a vase on the dining table—a visual reminder of the man she would rather forget.

He phoned mid-afternoon. She had run a bath—hoping to soothe her aching muscles after her run—and was blissfully immersed in scented bubbles when she heard the telephone. After the tenth ring she could stand it no longer, cursing as she wrapped a towel around her before padding barefoot down the hall, leaving a trail of foam in her wake.

The caller was annoyingly persistent, which meant that it was probably her mother, she thought grimly. It was less than six months since Judith had phoned from her home in France and dropped the bombshell that she had just married for the third time. Was it too soon for her mother to be ringing to announce her divorce? Anna wondered cynically as she snatched up the receiver.

'Anna, I hope I haven't disturbed you,' a familiar, heavily accented voice sounded in her ear, causing goose-bumps to prickle her skin so that she twitched her towel firmly in place.

'I was in the bath,' she replied shortly, 'and now I'm dripping water all over the carpet.'

In his hotel room Damon stretched out on the bed and closed his eyes as he pictured Anna—damp, pink-cheeked and wrapped in a towel. Possibly not even a towel, he mused, feeling the familiar stirring in his loins. Those gorgeous, lissom limbs would be satin-smooth, perhaps glistening with a few stray droplets of moisture. Her blonde hair would be piled on top of her head while stray tendrils framed her face. Hunger flared as he imagined himself releasing the pins so that it fell in a swathe of gold silk over her breasts. 'I'm sorry. Do you want to go and put something on?'

'It's all right; I've got a towel round me.'

'Ah, bath-sheet or hand-towel?' he enquired throatily.

'Does it matter?' Anna inhaled sharply and fought to control the quiver that ran through her at the sound of his sexy drawl. 'Did you want something, Damon—other than a description of the size of my towel?'

It was tempting to spell out in glorious detail *precisely* what he wanted, but Damon restrained himself. 'I have two tickets for the Royal Ballet tonight. I wondered if you would care to join me?'

His voice was deliberately light and neutral, as if he feared that she would accuse him of pressurising her. It was tempting, Anna admitted silently. He was tempting. She hesitated, her eyes drawn along the hallway to the dining room, where the roses he had sent her were reflected in the polished mahogany table. She felt as though she were balanced on the edge of a precipice and one wrong move could send her hurtling to her destruction.

'Why did you send me flowers?' she demanded huskily.

'They remind me of you—fragrant, fragile and infinitely beautiful,' he replied seriously. 'Don't you like them?'

'Of course I do—what woman doesn't love flowers?' she whispered as her body reacted to the smoky sensuality of his voice. But the thought of all the other women in his life sent her skidding back down to earth. Damon was well practised in the art of seduction. Did he send flowers to every blonde he was interested in? He must have an enormous florists' bill, she thought sardonically as common sense reasserted itself.

'I'm afraid I promised to babysit for a friend tonight and I can't let her down,' she lied. It seemed a foolproof excuse and she was just congratulating herself on her quick thinking when he spoke again.

'Perhaps I could help out? I'm good with children.'

Too late she recalled the gentle patience he'd shown on Zathos towards his little godson Theo. She'd been struck by his natural affinity with children and surprised by the idea that he would make a good father.

Next thing she would be canonising him, she thought impatiently.

'I don't think that would be a good idea, and I'm sure you don't want to waste your tickets. You'll have to flick through your little black book and find another partner for the evening. You must have several willing candidates to choose from,' she added cattily, dismayed at how much she hated the idea that she was just one in a long list of blondes in his phone book.

'Dozens,' he assured her blandly, 'but you're currently top of the list.'

'Lucky me,' she replied every bit as blandly, gently

placing the phone down before he had the chance to reply, and then spent the next ten minutes hovering in the hallway in case he should ring again. He didn't, and, berating herself for being a fool, she returned to her rapidly cooling bath water, any idea of relaxing blown to pieces.

She had been right to turn him down, she assured herself for the hundredth time. Instinct warned her that Damon was out of her league and although he fascinated her, she refused to risk her emotional security on a man who regarded women as nothing more than sexual playmates.

Several hours later she was beginning to wish she had accepted Damon's invitation.

'Hey, Anna, why aren't you drinking?'

The question was slurred and indistinct and Anna turned her head sharply to avoid a wave of alcoholic fumes. Tonight was rapidly turning into the evening from hell, she brooded darkly when Jack Bailey, star of a series of commercials for a popular brand of jeans, slid into the seat next to her.

'Here, waiter, more champagne,' Jack demanded. 'Do you know who this is?' he asked the waiter in a loud voice that caused heads to turn. 'This is Anna Christiansen, the most beautiful woman in the world—isn't that right, Anna?' He leered at her, his handsome face flushed from the effects of too much wine, and Anna stifled a groan.

Having refused Damon's invitation to the ballet, she'd been left facing a long, lonely evening and had jumped when her phone had rung again just after six, her frisson of anticipation quickly dissipating when she'd discovered that the call was from one of the models she had worked with in South Africa.

Dinner with friends, even if they were acquaintances rather than close confidantes, was better than a night in front of the TV, she had decided. And at least it would focus her mind on something other than a certain enigmatic Greek.

But at the restaurant it soon became apparent that the quiet meal she'd anticipated had developed into a full-blown social event. Friends of friends joined the party, the wine flowed and the group grew louder, attracting attention from other diners. Jack's drunken attempts to climb inside her dress were the last straw and she gave him an icy glare.

'Shut up, Jack,' she muttered irritably. 'Don't you think you've had enough to drink?'

Her acerbic comments merely caused the young actor to grin wolfishly and while she was endeavouring to remove his hand from her cleavage she felt a shiver run the length of her spine. It was the same feeling that she remembered from Kezia's dinner party and filled with foreboding, she slowly lifted her head.

Damon was sitting at a table some distance away. Even though her view was partly obscured by other diners, Anna instantly recognised him and her heart lurched as her gaze slid to his attractive companion. Was the woman number two on his list? she wondered bleakly as she stared at the stunning redhead by his side.

It was late in the evening and she guessed that Damon and his companion had come to the restaurant straight from the theatre. Doubtless the Royal Ballet's performance of *Swan Lake* had been spectacular she mused bleakly, wishing that she had found the courage to accept his invitation.

The fact that he'd had no problem finding another partner for the evening proved that she had been wise to decline, she told herself firmly. But she could not tear her eyes from him and she held her breath when he suddenly stiffened and glanced across the busy restaurant.

Even from a distance she registered his brief flare of surprise when he caught sight of her and she blushed, re-membering her earlier excuse that she was babysitting for a friend tonight. It was obvious that Damon was also recalling her lie. His gaze slid to Jack Bailey, who was slumped in a drunken stupor beside her, and his mouth curled into a dark smile before he deliberately returned his attention to his companion.

Damn him, she thought furiously. He wasn't her keeper. And so what if she had lied? Maybe now he would get the message that she didn't want to have anything to do with him.

But to her chagrin she found that she couldn't prevent her eyes from straying in his direction. He looked gorgeous—lean, dark and simmering with his own lethal brand of sexual magnetism. She wasn't the only woman in the room to have noticed him, either, she noted grimly as a quick scan of the restaurant revealed that most female eyes were focused on one man.

At that moment he looked up and trapped her gaze with his brooding stare. The hubbub of voices became muted and the other diners seemed to fade to the periphery of her vision, leaving nothing but Damon and the powerful electric current that flared between them.

Her reaction was instant and shockingly basic as heat coursed through her veins. Her breasts ached and a horrified glance revealed that her nipples were clearly visible through her clingy jersey top. He couldn't see from that distance, she consoled herself, but the sudden tension apparent in his shoulders warned her that he was well aware of the effect he had on her.

'Anna, we're going on to a club. Do you want to come?' Jack Bailey's voice sounded in her ear—as annoyingly persistent as a wasp, it at least gave her the excuse to break free from the spell that Damon had cast over her.

'No, thanks, I've had enough and I'm going home,' she replied curtly.

'Come on, don't be such a bore,' Jack muttered sulkily.

He staggered after her as she picked a route through the restaurant that carefully avoided going anywhere near Damon and his gorgeous dinner date. Outside it was bedlam. The restaurant was currently one of the most popular venues in London and the paparazzi had gathered in droves, desperate to snap shots of any celebrities.

The last thing she wanted was for pictures of her and Jack to be plastered across the front pages of tomorrow's tabloids, Anna thought grimly. For some reason the press were fascinated by her love life but she refused to be a pawn in their stupid game.

She retreated into a corner of the lobby, but Jack must have noticed and a moment later he joined her, his eyes glazed and his shirt buttons half undone as he trapped her against a wall with his arms on either side of her head.

'Okay, forget the club. We'll have our own private party, just you and me, baby. Do you want to come back to my place?' He swayed unsteadily and slumped forwards so that his full weight pinioned Anna against the wall. His breath was hot on her skin as he ground his lips on hers and his hands seemed to be everywhere, damp with sweat as they edged beneath her top.

Instantly she was transported back in time. Instead of Jack, it was her stepfather pushing her against the wall, laughing at her as she struggled to prevent him from touching her.

'Jack, get off me! Leave me alone.' Overwhelmed by panic and a growing feeling of claustrophobia, she gave a shrill cry and lashed out, her hand making sharp contact with his cheek.

'Bloody hell, you little vixen, what did you do that for?' Jack reared back, easing the pressure on her chest, and she gulped for air, her breath coming in short, shallow gasps. 'Everyone says you're a frigid bitch and now I know why,' he taunted, his sneering smile fading when a hand landed heavily on his shoulder.

'Do you need any help, Anna?'

Damon materialised in front of her, his dark eyes cold and merciless as he gripped Jack's arm, restraining the younger man with insulting ease. Anna would like to have made some flippant remark and shrugged off the incident but instead she nodded wordlessly.

She felt sick with a mixture of shame and fear. Nothing could have happened, she reminded herself impatiently. They were in the lobby of a busy restaurant and Jack couldn't have hurt her—forced her... She shuddered and closed her mind to the memories that had resurfaced. She didn't want to think, not now.

The restaurant manager appeared, frowning as he took in the scene. 'Shall I call the police?' he addressed Damon.

'No!' Anna's eyes were unconsciously pleading. The story would be fodder for the gutter press and she couldn't bear the humiliation of reading about her supposed relationship with Jack in tomorrow's downmarket papers.

'I don't think that will be necessary,' Damon answered, his gaze not leaving Anna's pale face. 'I'll leave you to deal with *him.*' He threw a scathing glance at Jack, whose initial bravado had disappeared and who was now swaying unsteadily on his feet. 'Plenty of black coffee, or a bucket of water over his head—I know which one I'd choose,' he told the manager with a grim smile. 'Is there another way out? The world's press seem to be camped on the front steps.'

'You can leave through the kitchens,' the manager said quickly. 'Come this way.'

'It's all right, I can take care of myself,' Anna muttered as her eyes flew from Damon to his beautiful redheaded companion who was plainly bemused by the scene.

The look on his face said it all. 'Do you really want to

step out there—' he gestured to the front of the restaurant where the paparazzi were assembled on the pavement '—looking like that?'

Before she could reply he spun her round and she gasped at the sight of her reflection in the mirror. Her hair had escaped its once-neat chignon and was hanging in rats' tails around her face, her lipstick was smeared over her chin, but it was her eyes, wild and overbright with unshed tears that gave away the fact that she was near breaking-point.

'The press would have a field day,' Damon told her tersely. He took his phone from his pocket. 'I'll have my driver meet us out back.'

She had no option but to comply, Anna acknowledged when Damon ushered her through the door leading to the kitchens. She half turned to say something but found that he had hung back and was speaking in a quiet undertone to his companion.

What must the other woman be thinking? She bit her lip and followed the restaurant manager through the back door, out into a narrow alley where they had to squeeze past the rubbish bins. She was so embarrassed she wanted to die and could not bring herself to look at Damon or his friend when a car pulled up in the alleyway and a uniformed chauffeur sprang out.

'There was really no need for you to end your evening,' she muttered. 'Ask your driver to drop me off on the main road and I'll take a cab home.'

It was Damon's companion who answered. 'It's really not a problem. I promised my husband that I would be back before midnight anyway,' she added with a smile. 'We don't want to upset him, do we, Damon?'

'Certainly not. Friend or not, I think Marc would feel justified in thumping me if I did not bring you back safely and on time,' he replied, his eyes glinting with amusement at

Anna's obvious confusion. 'Anna, I'd like to introduce you to Elaine Sotiriou. Her husband and I were at school together and I was lucky enough to persuade Marc to lend me his wife for the evening.'

'Yes, the ballet was wonderful. It's such a pity you'd already arranged to meet your friends,' Elaine said sympathetically. The car pulled up in a mews of tall Georgian houses and she leaned forwards to brush her lips against Damon's cheek. 'You're welcome to come in for coffee—both of you,' she added, giving Anna a gentle smile. 'My husband would love to meet you.'

'Another time perhaps,' Damon replied. 'I need to get Anna home.'

Anna opened her mouth to tell him that she was not his responsibility, remembered her ravaged appearance and thought better of it. If she was honest she couldn't wait to reach the quiet sanctuary of her flat. The incident with Jack had been unpleasant rather than traumatic but it had evoked memories of her stepfather that even now, after all this time, still had the power to disturb her.

She was silent for the twenty-minute drive across town, her body as tense as a coiled spring as she waited for Damon to comment on the fact that she had lied to him earlier. He said nothing, seemingly lost in his thoughts, and as the limousine swung into the parking area outside her flat she released her breath on a shaky sigh.

'Thanks for bringing me home and…everything.' Everything included rescuing her from Jack Bailey's drunken advances but she was too embarrassed to spell it out and slid out of the car with as much dignity as she could muster.

'I'll see you up.'

'There's no need.'

Reaction was setting in and she was unable to repress a shiver. Damon's mouth tightened. Did she have any idea how vulnerable she looked? he wondered. Her eyes were wide; the expression in their depths *bruised*, he noted grimly. He placed his hand lightly on her shoulder to guide her towards the steps and felt her flinch.

Surely she didn't think he would leap on her as her drunken dinner date had done? The thought was enough for him to remove his hand and he contented himself with following her closely up the two flights of stairs to her flat.

At the front door she paused and he took the key from her trembling fingers.

'Damon.'

He caught the note of desperation in her voice and his jaw tensed. 'I'll make the coffee while you repair the damage your lover inflicted. And then I promise I'll go,' he said steadily.

'Jack's not my lover.' Far from it, she thought with a shudder of revulsion. 'He's just a friend. Not even that really,' she admitted honestly. 'Dinner with a crowd of acquaintances seemed a safer option than…'

'Spending the evening with me,' Damon finished for her, watching the way her cheeks flooded with colour. Once again he was aware of a curious tug of protectiveness. Anneliese Christiansen was reputed to be worldly-wise and sophisticated—the Ice Princess who lured her many lovers with her cool beauty. But the woman standing before him reminded him of a frightened child and he had to restrain himself from drawing her into his arms.

Instinct warned him that if he touched her she would lash out like a cornered wildcat and he carefully kept his distance as he followed her into her flat and down the narrow passageway to the kitchen.

'Coffee, and then you have to go,' she told him, unable to keep the tremor from her voice as she filled the kettle and reached into the cupboard for cups. One slipped through her fingers and as it shattered on the floor she gave a cry and knelt to gather up the pieces.

'Leave it.'

She jumped at the harshness of his tone and stared up at him, blinking furiously. Damon caught the glint of her tears and felt his gut tighten.

'Go and get cleaned up,' he bade her quietly, taking her hand and drawing her to her feet. She still had a trace of lipstick smeared across her face and he wiped it with his thumb pad.

The moment he'd stepped into the lobby and seen her struggling in the arms of that drunken lout, who'd been pawing her all evening, he'd wanted to commit murder. He couldn't understand where this edge of possessiveness had come from, this urge to take care of her as if she were infinitely precious to him.

He barely knew her, he reminded himself impatiently as he pushed her gently out of the kitchen. Common sense warned him that Anna spelt trouble, in more ways than one. But for the last two months he'd been unable to forget her and even now, when she was ashen and achingly vulnerable, he still desired her more than any woman he'd ever known.

Anna tore her gaze from Damon and shot into the bathroom where she quickly locked the door behind her. She felt dirty, sullied by Jack Bailey's touch, and with swift, almost desperate movements she stripped out of her clothes and dived into the shower.

She quickly scrubbed her body, all the while conscious of faint noises from the kitchen. Damon was probably making coffee as promised.

Suddenly she was fifteen again, listening to the sound of her stepfather's footsteps outside the bathroom door and knowing that he would be there, lurking on the landing when she emerged. He had always had a legitimate reason, of course, but she shuddered at the memory of his sly grin and the way his eyes had followed her when she'd fled to her bedroom.

This had to stop, she told herself sharply. She stepped out of the shower cubicle and huddled in the folds of a towel. She wasn't fifteen any more, she was twenty-five—a grown woman with a successful career and no one could hurt her, certainly not her mother's second husband Philip Stone.

'You're such a pretty girl, Annie. Not even a girl any more. I've noticed how you're developing into a woman.'

'Shut up, Phil, or I'll tell Mum.'

'Tell her what, Annie? I was only saying that you've blossomed into a real stunner. I bet lots of men like to look at you. I know I do.'

'No! Anna's eyes flew open and she stared at herself in the mirror, her face twisted with revulsion at the memories of her stepfather. Phil was in the past. She hadn't seen him since she'd left home at seventeen—preferring to struggle on her own rather than live under the same roof as her tormentor. Her stepfather's sly sexual innuendos had sickened her but when he had started to try and touch her—a hand on her thigh or a playful pat on her bottom, carried out in the guise of jolly Uncle Phil—she'd known that she had to leave.

Confiding in her mother had never been an option. After years of depression brought about by the failure of her first marriage, Judith had finally been happy again and Anna had been unable to bring herself to ruin that happiness. Instead she'd kept quiet about Phil's unhealthy fascination with his stepdaughter and had assured Judith that she was moving into a flat with friends. Life had been tough for a while, but she'd survived and along the way she'd learned that trust was for fools.

Her mother's marriage to Phil had eventually also ended in divorce. She didn't know the reasons why and had never asked. Despite Judith's pleadings, she'd refused to return home to the house that she had come to hate. She had a new life, earning the kind of money she'd only ever dreamed of, and she'd made a solemn vow that she would never give up her independence for anyone.

'Anna, your coffee's getting cold.' Damon's terse voice sounded through the bathroom door, his tone laced with an underlying concern.

'All right—I'm just coming.' Her thick towelling robe fell past her knees, concealing her curves. She wanted no opportunity for misunderstanding, she thought grimly as she belted it tightly around her waist. She might have allowed Damon into her flat, but coffee was the only thing on offer.

He was the most gorgeous, sexy, charismatic man she had ever met and she was still reeling from her unexpected reaction to his kiss. But forewarned was forearmed and in the spirit of her self-preservation she was determined that it wouldn't happen again.

CHAPTER FIVE

WHEN Anna entered the sitting room she found Damon sprawled on the sofa, his long legs stretched out in front of him and his arms folded behind his head. He had discarded his jacket and tie and unfastened the top couple of shirt buttons to reveal a sprinkling of wiry black chest hair.

To Anna's mind he seemed to dominate the small sitting room, his brazen masculinity a stark contrast to the ultra feminine décor of her flat.

'I see you've made yourself at home,' she commented pithily as she retreated to the armchair furthest away from him. He had switched on the stereo player and the CD he'd selected was one of her current favourites—easy listening that soothed her rattled nerves. He looked as though he was settled for the night, she noted darkly, her senses suddenly on high alert when he gave her one of his devastating smiles.

'Your coffee's here,' he murmured, gesturing to the tray he had set on the low table in front of him. 'And I made some sandwiches. I noticed you didn't eat much at the restaurant.'

'My God, don't tell me you were spying on me. I can look after myself, you know.'

'Yes, I noticed.'

The softly spoken comment caused her to blush as she recalled how he had rescued her from Jack Bailey's clutches.

Anxious to avoid his quizzical gaze, she lifted the napkin from the tray and discovered a pile of sandwiches neatly arranged on a plate.

He'd even taken the trouble to trim off the crusts, she noted. She was so used to fending for herself that the simple gesture caused a prickling sensation behind her eyelids. It was a long time since she'd felt cared for and for some ridiculous reason she felt like crying. With a faint air of desperation she bit into a sandwich. It was true that she had barely touched her dinner and she was surprised to find she was hungry.

'I can't manage all of them,' she muttered stubbornly when she lifted her eyes to find him watching her eat, a look of smug satisfaction on his face. Was he always right? Damn him.

'Come and sit over here and I'll help you out,' he replied, patting the empty space on the sofa. It seemed churlish to refuse and she reluctantly moved next to him, perching awkwardly on the edge of the cushion, her body tensed and ready for instant flight.

'I had no idea you were so domesticated,' she commented coolly as she helped herself to another sandwich.

Damon shrugged. 'I don't have a problem dealing with the mundane things in life. Like you, I value my independence and at home I employ the minimum of staff.' He paused fractionally and then added, 'My wife was a great believer in equality between the sexes and she made it clear from day one of our marriage that she wouldn't run around after me like a traditional Greek wife.'

Anna was aware of a peculiar buzzing sensation in her ears. The room tilted alarmingly and she inhaled sharply, desperate to drag oxygen into her lungs. She couldn't faint; it would be so…pathetic, she told herself furiously. Her sandwich suddenly seemed to be made of cardboard and she had to force herself to swallow her mouthful.

'I didn't know you had a wife,' she said sharply when she could trust herself to speak. She felt physically sick as a variety of emotions threatened to overwhelm her, chiefly anger, she acknowledged grimly. If he was married, what was he doing here in her flat, and why had he kissed her?

God, did he really think he was so irresistible that she would agree to become his mistress, knowing that he had a wife in the background?

'She died eight years ago.' The statement was flat and unemotional and Anna's startled gaze flew to his face.

'I'm sorry, I didn't know,' she mumbled, unaware that he could read each fleeting emotion that crossed her face— shock and confusion mixed with sympathy and a faint hint of relief. 'Was it an accident, or was she ill?'

'A tragic mix of both—Eleni suffered from asthma but it was controlled by medication, or so we believed. There was no indication in the days before her death that her condition had worsened. She was her usual, vibrant self when I left on a business trip,' Damon explained. 'She was an artist and it seems that while she was alone in her studio at the top of the house she suffered a particularly severe attack and couldn't get to her inhaler in time. By the time the housekeeper found her it was too late, she was already dead.'

'Oh, God! How awful. You must miss her,' Anna whispered.

'It was a long time ago,' he offered quietly. 'Life moves on—it has to. But it took a long time to come to terms with the tragedy of a young life so cruelly taken, especially when Eleni had so much to live for.' He hesitated fractionally, as if he was about to say something else, but then continued— 'Perhaps losing her so unexpectedly is the reason that I'm determined to seize every opportunity. Life isn't a dress rehearsal,' he murmured, staring at her intently with eyes that were so dark she felt as though she could drown in their depths.

'I'm so sorry,' she repeated helplessly. The words seemed totally inadequate and, overwhelmed by emotion, she placed her hand on his arm, wanting to comfort him. Damon reached out and ran a finger lightly down her cheek before cupping her chin and tilting her face to his.

'Don't,' he bade huskily as a solitary tear over-spilled and slid down her face. 'You have an unexpectedly compassionate heart, *pedhaki mou.*'

He couldn't disguise the faint note of surprise in his tone and she jerked back as if he had slapped her.

'What did you expect—that I was the spoilt, haughty supermodel the press like to portray?' she demanded sharply. 'The Ice Princess with a retinue of willing lovers? Is that why you're here, Damon— You assumed I'd agree to a meaningless sexual liaison with no messy emotions to screw it up?'

She broke off, unable to hide the hurt in her voice. Damon had earned a reputation as a playboy with a penchant for nubile blondes, and she was just one in a long line of women who had attracted his passing interest. But beneath the surface he was obviously a man capable of deep emotions. She didn't doubt that he had loved his wife. She'd heard evidence of it in his voice when he'd spoken of Eleni; had seen it in the sudden softening of his expression when he'd mentioned her name.

It was ridiculous to feel so *betrayed,* she told herself angrily. And obscene to feel jealous of the young Greek girl who had captured Damon's heart and whose life had been cut so tragically short.

'If I'd simply wanted sex, there are a number of options I could have chosen,' he growled, the rigid line of his jaw warning her that he was struggling to keep his anger in check. He didn't add that any one of those options would have been easier than pursuing a woman who seemed hell-bent on rejecting him.

If he was frank, he *had* believed that Anna would succumb to the undeniable attraction between them with a minimum of effort on his part. He had been guilty as charged of believing the gossip about her numerous, short-lived affairs and he was honest enough to accept that initially he'd simply wanted to take her to bed.

Okay, he still did, he acknowledged impatiently. His desire for Anna was fast becoming an obsession. He would like nothing better than to unfasten the belt of her robe, part the bulky material and discover her slender curves with his hands and mouth.

Instinct told him that her resistance would be minimal. Even now, the anger mirrored in her stunning blue eyes was mixed with a shimmer of awareness that she could not hide. It would be easy to close the distance between them and capture her mouth, initiate a sensual exploration until her defences crumbled and she responded to his kiss with the desire that he sensed matched his own.

Something held him back; the shadows in her eyes and the slight tremor of her bottom lip that she sought to control by catching the soft flesh with her teeth. On a physical level there was no doubt in his mind that Anna would respond to him. In his thirty-eight years he had enjoyed numerous sexual liaisons, some casual and others that had meant more to him. His marriage had meant the world, but Eleni was dead and in the years since her death he had found no reason to deny himself the pleasure of female company.

He knew without conceit that he possessed both the skill and sensitivity to ensure Anna's sexual pleasure, but mentally she would withdraw even further behind the barriers she had erected. A small voice in his head urged him to simply take what he wanted and to hell with the consequences, but he glimpsed the naked vulnerability in her eyes and realised with a jolt of surprise that he would hate to hurt her.

'We seem to have got off to a bad start,' he ventured quietly. 'I think we both harboured preconceived ideas about each other. Can't we wipe the slate clean and start again?'

Anna stared at him, unable to disguise her confusion. 'Why do you want to?' she demanded suspiciously.

'Because you intrigue me more than any woman I've ever met,' he replied honestly. He trapped her gaze, his eyes clear and candid as if he wanted to prove that he had no hidden agenda. 'And because you are so very lovely, Anna *mou*, that I can't keep my eyes off you. Even when I'm not with you, you dominate my thoughts.'

How did she respond to that? Anna wondered wildly as her heart lurched in her chest. He was practised in the art of seduction but his words held a ring of sincerity about them, rather than a glib statement designed to fool her. Dared she trust him? Wasn't he just the same as every other man she'd met— fascinated by her image but uninterested in the real Anna?

'Someone once told me that men would only ever want me for one thing,' she burst out, her stark admission taking them both by surprise. She didn't know what had induced her to reveal the poison that festered in her brain and her eyes darkened when she recalled her stepfather's taunts.

'You're a little sex-pot Annie, the embodiment of every male fantasy. Forget that rubbish about respecting your mind—every man who ever looks at you will only be interested in your body.'

'You don't believe that, surely?' Damon demanded. The *someone* she'd spoken of had obviously set out to wreck her self-esteem and it seemed they'd done a good job. 'Your looks are only one part of you, teamed with intelligence, wit and an obvious compassion for others.' He cupped her face once more and stared into her eyes. 'Who was he?' he demanded harshly. 'Who hurt you so badly that he made you doubt your self-worth?'

'It doesn't matter,' Anna mumbled, desperately trying to evade his gaze that seemed to burn into her soul. 'He's in the past.'

'Yet he still exerts power over you. Was he a lover who resented it when you ended the relationship and sought to destroy your confidence?' Damon saw the shudder that ran through her, glimpsed the trace of fear in her eyes and his jaw tightened. 'Did he *hurt* you—physically?'

The thought was enough to make him want to commit murder. He was shocked by the strength of his fury, but the idea that anyone could lay a finger on her in anger filled him with revulsion.

'Just leave it, Damon; it's not important.' Anna jerked out of his grasp and jumped to her feet, sending the contents of her coffee-cup flying. 'Damn it, now see what you've made me do,' she snapped as she attempted to blot the pool of coffee with a napkin. 'I think it's time you left.'

She didn't want to talk about the past and was already regretting her impulsive statement. How could she convince Damon that she was in control of her emotions when she'd allowed him to glimpse the chinks in her armour?

Damon wisely said no more as he slung his jacket over his shoulder and followed her along the hallway to the front door. He sensed the fierce tension that gripped her, noted the way her eyes seemed too big for her heart-shaped face, and once again he was overwhelmed with the urge to protect her. Far from being the Ice Princess that the press portrayed, she was near to breaking-point, so emotionally fragile that he could not prevent himself from reaching out to smooth her hair back from her temple.

'I mean you no harm, Anna, I swear it,' he vowed in a low tone.

The shimmer of tears caused his gut to clench and he watched as she waged a silent battle in her head. Murmuring a husky imprecation, he halted the trail of moisture that trickled down her cheek with his thumb pad and lowered his head to brush his lips gently across hers.

She stiffened but did not pull away and he deepened the kiss a little, allowing his tongue to make a tender exploration of the contours of her mouth. Still she didn't reject him, but neither did she respond—just stood, trembling, her body poised for flight.

His one thought was to ease the rigid tension that gripped her. She'd had one hell of a night, he acknowledged grimly as he recalled her struggles with the drunken lout in the restaurant. No wonder she looked as though she would shatter at the lightest touch.

With infinite care he stroked his tongue against the tight line of her lips and felt a quiver run through her. He hadn't expected her to respond, but to his delight she hesitantly opened her mouth to allow him access to the sweetness within. Triumph flooded through him, tempered with a degree of caution. It was tempting to wrap his arms around her and draw her close but he forced himself to clench his hands by his sides so that the only contact between them was mouth on mouth, the gentle sweep of his tongue as he deepened the kiss until it became a sensual tasting that he wanted never to stop.

When at last he lifted his head, Anna could only stare at him, too stunned to utter a word. She was shaking; not through fear or revulsion, but with the desperate need to have him draw her up against the hard wall of his chest. She wanted to feel him, wanted to revel in the brush of his thighs against hers. She wanted to touch him and have him touch her, but now he was stepping away from her, ending the kiss that had shattered her belief that she would never feel sexual desire.

'I'm going to be out of the country for a few days and it's

possible I may not be back in time for your race, so I'll wish you good luck now,' he said in a matter-of-fact tone as he turned and opened the front door.

'Thank you—I'll see you…some time,' Anna murmured dazedly.

'You can count on it, *pedahaki mou*.'

The gleam in his eyes promised her they were at the start of a journey that could only have one destination. The knowledge should have sent her running for cover but instead she was filled with a strange sense of anticipation.

She wanted him, she admitted, feeling a tremor run through her. But it was so new and unexpected after all the years when she had convinced herself she was cold and passionless. Damon had just proved that she was neither, but the barriers in her head had built up over a long time and the thought of lowering them terrified her.

She waited until he had disappeared down the stairs and then closed the door, returned to the sitting room and collected the tray as if she were running on autopilot. A glance at the clock showed that it was past midnight.

She had a magazine shoot booked for early the next morning, followed by another training session at the track. Sleep was imperative but proved elusive as she tossed and turned beneath the sheets. Damon, and her response to his kiss, filled her mind. But her dreams were fractured with images of him as a loving husband whose heart belonged for ever to his tragic young wife.

The charity half-marathon around Hyde Park attracted fevered media interest, due mainly to the number of celebrities taking part. Spurred on by the cheering crowd, Anna crossed the finish line in under three hours and felt euphoric at the knowledge that she had raised a huge amount of money for the children's charity.

She spent the next day quietly relaxing and only ventured out to the health spa for a massage, which worked wonders on her aching muscles. Early evening saw her indulging in a long, hot soak until her peace was shattered by the strident peal of the doorbell. She was half inclined to ignore it and lay back and closed her eyes, but the caller was persistent and, cursing beneath her breath, she hauled herself out of the bath, wrapped a towel around her, sarong-style, and marched down the hall.

'You have a habit of getting me out of the bath,' she snapped, fighting to control the frantic race of her pulse when she opened the door a fraction and discovered Damon leaning indolently against the frame.

'If only that were true, *pedhaki mou,*' he murmured throatily, his dark eyes glinting with amusement and another more disturbing emotion as his gaze slid over her damp body, barely concealed beneath the towel. 'But it's a habit I'd very much like to acquire.'

Damn him. He was incorrigible, Anna thought, unable to prevent her lips from twitching. She had never met anyone like him before and, although she was loath to admit it, she'd missed him.

'What do you want, Damon?'

'To offer my congratulations,' he said blandly. 'I only arrived back in England an hour ago and I've come straight from the airport, but I heard the news of your success in the charity race and I'm delighted to be able to give you this.'

He handed her a cheque made out to the charity and Anna's eyes widened as she stared at the figure scrawled in black ink.

'You weren't joking, then?' she questioned faintly.

'Did you honestly doubt my commitment?'

There was no answer to that and Anna was suddenly conscious that she couldn't expect him to remain on the doorstep indefinitely. Slowly she opened the door wider for him to enter and clutched her towel to her as if it were a life raft thrown to a drowning man.

He'd made no mention of her joining him for dinner, as he'd threatened when he'd first agreed to sponsor her. Perhaps he had forgotten, or was no longer interested, she thought a shade bleakly.

'The charity will be overwhelmed by your generosity,' she told him huskily as she glanced again at the cheque. 'I can't quite believe it, but I'm surprised you've given it to me now.'

'Before I've held you to your agreement to have dinner with me, you mean?' His expression was one of gentle amusement, as if he understood the reasons for her uncertainty. 'I was rather hoping that you would agree to dine with me because you want to, rather than seeing it as a form of blackmail,' he added, plainly remembering her furious accusation on the night of Kezia's dinner party.

Sneaky didn't begin to describe him. It was little wonder that he had a reputation as the most wily man ever to set foot inside a boardroom, she thought darkly. In the interests of self-preservation she ought to tell him to get lost but the words wouldn't come and instead she stared up at him, the inner battle she was waging evident in the sapphire darkness of her eyes.

'Dinner seems the least I can do when you've been so incredibly…kind,' she responded at last, colour stealing into her cheeks at the way his eyebrows lifted quizzically. His look told her that *kind* was not a word usually associated with Damon Kouvaris, yet she didn't doubt his compassion.

'I'm glad to hear it. You've got half an hour,' he told her cheerfully, striding down the hall and into the sitting room as if he owned the place.

'Do you mean…you want us to have dinner *tonight?*' She

padded down the hall after him, a frown forming on her brow. 'But I'm still recovering from the race. I'm too tired!'

'It's only dinner, *pedhaki mou,* unless you were planning something a little more *energetic?*'

'Slapping you is the only thing that springs to mind,' she said grittily, her cheeks on fire. 'Tonight will be fine. At least it gets it out of the way.' With that she gripped her towel tightly round her and stormed out of the room, her temper not improved by the sound of his mocking laughter following her along the hall.

CHAPTER SIX

IN AN effort to disguise her nervousness, Anna selected a midnight-blue couture dress for her dinner date with Damon. The stark simplicity of the style conveyed the impression of cool sophistication, especially when teamed with a few discreet pieces of jewellery—sapphire and diamond earrings and a matching bracelet on her wrist.

With her hair swept into an elegant chignon and the addition of killer heels, she looked every inch the confident career woman. She could only pray that nobody would notice the slight tremor of her hands when she followed Damon across the foyer of his hotel.

'Where are we going?' she queried with a frown when he ushered her into the lift. 'I assumed the dining room is on the ground floor.'

'It is, but we're not eating there,' he replied with a smile that did nothing to allay her apprehension.

Anna surveyed him suspiciously as the lift whisked them towards the upper floors. She had already made her feelings clear when he'd informed her that they would be dining at his hotel rather than a restaurant. Now what? Perhaps the hotel had a dining area in the roof garden, she pondered, but she didn't relish the prospect of sitting in the rain.

'I need to shower and change, and then I thought we'd

dine in the privacy of my suite,' he explained cheerfully as he led the way along a corridor and threw open the door leading to a large, luxuriously appointed room.

Anna glanced around warily, noting the elegant furnishings and the small dining table set for two. At the far end of the room was a door, which she guessed led to Damon's bedroom. It was that last thought that caused her to stop dead.

Damon glanced at her, his smile fading as he noticed her icy expression. 'Do you have any objections?'

'Dozens, the main one being that you tricked me.'

'In what way?' he demanded forcefully. 'You agreed to have dinner with me of your own free will.'

'I assumed we would be spending the evening in a busy restaurant, not in your room.'

'It's the penthouse suite, not the broom cupboard. What's the real issue, here Anna?' he demanded, his eyes narrowing when she shied away from him. 'Do you honestly think I brought you here with the intention of seducing you?'

'Didn't you?'

He was silent for so long that she lifted her eyes to stare at him, wondering what he was thinking. Too late she realised that the rigid set of his jaw gave a clue to the level of his anger. He was furious, his nostrils flaring as he sought to control his temper, and Anna realised with growing unease that she had insulted him unforgivably.

'Damon, I—' She broke off and extended her hand in a helpless gesture of contrition.

'Why don't you go back down and wait for me in the main lounge?' he suggested, his clipped tone indicating that he couldn't care less if she caught the next bus home. 'I'll meet you in twenty minutes and we'll have a drink while you're deciding whether you're willing to risk sitting in a public restaurant with me.'

He swung round and strode away from her, pausing briefly in the doorway leading to his room. 'Tell me, Anna, what are you so afraid of?'

There was no simple answer to that and she shook her head in silence, utterly beyond speech. How could she possibly begin to explain the mental damage her stepfather had inflicted? The misery of every school holiday spent trying to evade a man who had delighted in taunting her with revolting suggestions of what he would like to do to her.

She had moved out as soon as possible, before Phil had had a chance to carry out the abuses he'd threatened. But, as she'd been an impressionable teenager, her imagination had proved her worst enemy and the nightmares had haunted her for years.

'Are you afraid of me?' His voice was so gruff that she could almost believe she had hurt him.

Damon was nothing like her stepfather, she acknowledged. He might have a reputation as a playboy, but she knew instinctively that he would never physically harm her. Emotionally it was a different matter, but she couldn't bear the troubled look in his eyes and sought to reassure him.

'No,' she replied quietly.

He said no more, but she sensed a release in the fierce tension that gripped him. With a curt nod he entered his bedroom and closed the door firmly behind him.

Anna spent the next few minutes torn with indecision. Should she go downstairs and wait for him as he had suggested, or stay until he emerged from his room and try to seek his forgiveness? She had been unbelievably rude, she accepted grimly. This was a man who had just donated an astonishing amount of money to the children's hospice and she'd treated him as if he were Jack the Ripper.

A discreet knock on the door made the decision for her.

'I've come to clear away the table. Mr Kouvaris phoned

down to say that it's no longer required,' the bellboy explained.

'Wait. Actually there's been another change of plan and we'd like to have dinner up here after all,' Anna said. 'Is that still possible?'

'Anything's possible for Mr Kouvaris,' the bellboy replied seriously. 'Will the order be the same as before?'

'Yes, thank you.' She didn't know what dishes Damon had selected from the menu and, if she was honest, she didn't care. She just prayed she was doing the right thing and that her actions wouldn't further incite his anger.

She spent another ten minutes anxiously pacing the carpet while her tension increased to screaming pitch. A waiter arrived pushing a loaded trolley and she watched as he rearranged the cutlery and opened the wine, his precise attention to detail shredding her nerves. The faint snick of the door had her swinging round, her eyes wide with a mixture of uncertainty and bravado when Damon strolled through from his bedroom.

'Would you like me to pour the wine?' The waiter's eyes moved from her to Damon and in the ensuing pause, which seemed to last a lifetime, she discovered that she was holding her breath.

'I thought it would be nice to eat here after all,' she said quickly, flushing beneath Damon's quizzical stare.

'Good,' he murmured at last and nodded to the waiter to fill their glasses. He moved purposefully towards her, tall, dark and utterly devastating in superbly tailored black trousers and matching shirt. His hair was still damp from his shower and Anna noted the way it curled onto his collar. He exuded a simmering, sexual magnetism and she quivered when he came to stand in front of her, the scent of his cologne mixed with the fresh tang of soap, setting her senses on fire.

'What made you change your mind?'

She couldn't begin to tell him of the war that was waging inside her and shook her head helplessly.

'I thought it was a woman's prerogative?' she whispered, unaware of the stark vulnerability in her eyes.

He waited a heartbeat, his eyes dark and unfathomable while he studied her tense expression, and then he nodded and smiled at her so that his teeth gleamed white against his olive gold skin.

'Of course it is, *pedhaki mou*. I don't know about you, but I'm starving. Let's eat.'

It quickly became apparent that Damon was not a man to hold a grudge. He had every right to be annoyed with her, Anna acknowledged, but from the moment they took their places at the table he seemed determined to help her relax.

Witty, amusing and fiercely intelligent, he could charm the birds from the trees, she thought wryly. Dinner had been out of this world. She'd already eaten more than she should, but he tempted her to dessert—cheesecake with fresh raspberries and a summer berry coulis that tantalised her taste buds.

He kept their conversation deliberately light. They discussed the latest film release from a director they both admired and discovered a shared taste in modern authors. It was a long time since she had felt so at ease on a date, Anna mused as she finished her wine and shook her head when he offered to refill her glass.

She rarely drank alcohol and the glass of Chablis had left her feeling mellow and just the tiniest bit light-headed. It wasn't an unpleasant feeling, but she was wary of losing the tight grip on her control, especially with Damon around. Not that she did not trust him, she acceded; it was herself and her wayward response to the undisguised hunger in his eyes that worried her.

'Are you sure I can't persuade you to indulge in another slice of cheesecake?'

'Absolutely not!' She had a feeling that he could persuade her to indulge in a number of things that she wouldn't have dreamed of with any other man, but her slender figure was her fortune and she was grateful for her iron will-power. 'I can see that I'm going to have to run another thirteen miles tomorrow as it is,' she quipped lightly.

She left him pouring the coffee and wandered over to the window to stare out at the view of Marble Arch and Hyde Park beyond. The park was shrouded in black velvet but the surrounding streets were teeming with traffic, the car headlights winking like frenetic fireflies in the darkness. It was home, the sights and sounds comfortingly familiar, and Anna gave an unconscious sigh of pleasure.

'Do you enjoy living in London?'

She turned to find that Damon had moved to stand beside her and her senses leapt when he placed his hand lightly on the small of her back. The gesture was in no way threatening and a quiver ran through her. To her astonishment she realised that she longed for him to slide his arm around her waist and draw her up against the hard length of his body.

'I love it,' she replied hastily. 'Even during the bad times, after I'd left school and was struggling to find somewhere to live, I never considered moving away. It's a wonderful city and I'm proud that it's my home.'

'So where did you spend your childhood?' he asked, captivated by her enthusiasm.

'When my parents were together we lived in a house in Notting Hill,' she explained, wistfully recalling the past. 'It was an incredibly happy time. I used to think that my dad was the cleverest, funniest, most wonderful person in the world; he was so charming and good-looking. Unfortunately I wasn't the only female to think so,' she added dryly. 'After the divorce Mum couldn't keep up with the mortgage repayments and the house had to be sold. She and I moved into a flat and Lars lived a few streets away with his new wife and her children.'

'I suppose it at least meant you were able to see your father as often as you liked.'

'The access agreement was once a month, but Marion, Dad's second wife, didn't like me going to their house,' she told him flatly. 'She said I unsettled her two little girls but what she really meant was that I unsettled her. She couldn't stand the fact that I had a place in Dad's life.

'In my experience the whole step-parent, stepchild relationship is a minefield of resentment and jealousy,' she burst out, surprising them both with her sudden bitterness. 'If I'm sure of one thing, it's that I will never get involved with a man who has baggage.'

'Baggage?'

'Children,' she elaborated when Damon frowned. 'My stepmother did her best to destroy my relationship with my father, although ultimately he was the one who decided to break off contact. But I never want to be in the position where someone I care about feels that he has to choose between me and any children he might have from a previous relationship.'

'But surely there are thousands of couples in that situation for whom it works well?' Damon argued. 'Just because your own experiences were unhappy, it doesn't mean that it can't work with a little give and take on all sides.'

'Perhaps,' Anna said with a shrug, 'but it can also be a breeding ground for misery and heartache. I'm sorry, but, as you've probably guessed, it's a subject I feel strongly about,' she murmured huskily when Damon stared at her. He had tensed, his face as hard as if it had been sculpted from marble, but she had no idea what had disturbed him so strongly.

'Your childhood obviously left some serious scars—understandably when you lost your father and your home at such an impressionable age,' he said quietly. 'What about your mother—were you happy living with her? I imagine your financial circumstances were reduced.'

'We were broke,' Anna said with a harsh laugh. 'Before her marriage, my mother had been a brilliant musician with a promising career ahead of her, but she gave it all up to support my father in his various, and mostly unsuccessful, business ventures.

'She sacrificed everything for him,' she added bitterly. 'When he left us, she couldn't cope. She had some sort of breakdown and that's when I was sent away to school. Fortunately my grandmother had left an annuity to pay for my schooling.

'I loved my time at Braebourne Ladies College. I felt safe there,' she admitted, so quietly that he only just caught her words.

It was a strange thing to say and Damon frowned. Had there been times during her childhood when she hadn't felt safe? And whom had she been afraid of? Not her father, surely? From the way she had spoken of him, he guessed that she had adored Lars Christiansen and been devastated by his cruel desertion.

It was small wonder that she had such an issue with trust, he thought grimly. She was prickly and defensive but her father's seeming rejection of her in favour of his new wife and children had seeded the expectation that all men would let her down. Already she was edging away from him, clearly regretting the impulse that had led her to confide in him.

He wanted to draw her into his arms and hold her close, Damon acknowledged. He wanted to reassure her that he would never knowingly hurt her in any way.

The realisation caused him to frown. What was he thinking? His whole reason for coming to England and seeking her out had been to persuade her into his bed and keep her there until his hunger for her had been satiated. And how could he possibly hope to win her trust now, when there were issues in his life that he had deliberately kept from her?

It wasn't that he had set out to deceive her, he brooded when he joined her on the sofa and took a gulp of his coffee. But in the years since Eleni's death he had made a conscious decision to keep his private life separate from his family situation. He had never found the need to explain his commitments to his various mistresses; his life was neatly compartmentalised and he liked it that way.

He didn't even understand why he had told Anna about his marriage. Perhaps it was because he wanted to prove that there was more to him than his reputation as a wealthy playboy portrayed? But if that was the reason, it hadn't worked. He was no nearer to winning her trust and if he was scrupulously honest, he didn't deserve it when his motives had been triggered solely by lust.

Stifling an impatient sigh, he leaned back against the cushions and felt her stiffen. He could feel her watching him; surreptitious little glances when she thought he wasn't looking. But he was aware of the way her gaze focused on his mouth, aware of how her small, pink tongue suddenly darted out to moisten her lips. Desire pierced him, so savage that every muscle in his body clenched, and he strove to control the urge to plunder those soft lips with his own.

Walking away while he still had the chance no longer seemed to be an option, he acknowledged heavily. He'd never felt like this before; it was new and faintly terrifying, which was another alien emotion to him. He had never been afraid in his life, but as he recalled her fierce avowal that she would never become involved with a man with *baggage* his gut twisted and he tore his gaze from her to stare moodily at the blank television screen.

Anna drained her coffee and shifted edgily on the sofa. Damon seemed to be lost in his thoughts and, from the strained silence that had fallen, she could only assume that those thoughts were not happy ones. She was relieved when he activated the remote to switch on the television. At least forcing her brain to concentrate on the late evening news programme prevented her from dwelling on the intoxicating warmth of his thigh pressing lightly against hers.

The final part of the bulletin was devoted to coverage of the charity marathon and the work of the charity she had raised money for and she leaned forward slightly, her heart leaping when the presenter explained that the children's hospice was set to open ahead of target, thanks to the huge amount of funds raised from the race. The film then showed the vast crowd that had congregated in Hyde Park for the race the day before and she grimaced when her image flashed onto the screen.

'Oh, God, I hadn't realised that my running shorts were so, well…*short*,' she groaned, hectic colour flooding her cheeks. 'Over a thousand competitors took part, yet the cameraman seems to have spent the entire race fixated with my derrière.'

Beside her she felt Damon relax and she watched in fascination as his mouth curved into a slow smile.

'I have a certain amount of sympathy with him; he's only human, after all,' he said dulcetly, 'and it is a particularly delightful derrière, Anna *mou*.'

At his words, she snapped her head round, indignation warring with a strong desire to burst out laughing. He was the most outrageous flirt she had ever met, but the urge to slap him was lost before the lambent warmth of his gaze.

The tension between them returned with a vengeance, but

now it was laced with a degree of sexual awareness that she could neither ignore nor deny. Her breath caught in her throat and she could feel the erratic jerk of her pulse when he trailed a finger lightly down her cheek.

'Exquisite,' he breathed softly, suddenly sounding very Greek. He lowered his head, almost as if he had no control over his movements, and Anna watched, wide-eyed, as his mouth descended to claim her lips in a sweetly evocative caress.

This was dangerous, her brain warned when he lifted his head almost immediately and stared into her eyes. This was the very scenario she had hoped to avoid, and the reason she had wanted to dine in a restaurant rather than in Damon's private suite. Her experiences with her stepfather had taught her to avoid situations where she could be at risk, but, although she was alone with Damon, it wasn't fear that made her tremble.

She surveyed him warily when he slid his hand to her nape and released the clip that secured her chignon. Her hair fell in a heavy swathe of pale gold silk around her shoulders and she heard his low murmur of appreciation as he threaded his fingers through the silky strands. Far from terrifying her, the burning heat of his gaze filled her with a wild sense of excitement, and when he lowered his head once more she parted her lips to welcome the gentle exploration of his tongue.

It was soft and sensuous, but it wasn't enough. For the first time in her life she wanted more and she urged closer, winding her arms around his neck in the desperate hope that he would deepen the kiss.

Damon hesitated fractionally, afraid that he was rushing her, but the tentative stroke of her tongue against his lips shattered the remnants of his self-control and he increased the pressure of his mouth on hers to a level that was flagrantly erotic. He was aware of the slight tremor that ran through her and half expected her to draw back, but she leaned into him, one hand sliding down to rest over his heart thudding painfully in his chest.

She could hardly fail to realise the effect she was having on him, he acknowledged derisively. Not when his arousal was a throbbing, burgeoning force pushing against her hip. He needed to exert control over his rampaging hormones, but she had tormented his every waking thought for the past couple of months, invaded his dreams so that he'd woken hard and hot and as frustrated as hell. Who could blame him for seizing the sudden glimpse of heaven she was now offering?

Anna offered no resistance when Damon wrapped his arms around her and hauled her up against the hard wall of his chest. Desire was a potent force, she acknowledged with the tiny part of her brain still capable of conscious thought. She was overwhelmed by the feelings flooding through her. After so many years of imposing a rigid control over her emotions, it was a relief to discover that she was a normal woman, with normal sexual urges, although rather more disturbing to realise that it was only Damon who was able to arouse them.

When his hand skimmed her ribcage and then gently cupped her breast, heat flooded her and she closed her eyes, blotting out everything but the feel of his mouth on hers. The stroke of his thumb pad across her nipple caused an exquisite sensation that was new and wondrous and made her long for him to slide her dress from her shoulders. She wanted to feel him, skin on skin, his mouth to follow the path of his hands, and with a little murmur of frustration she cupped his face and kissed him with all the pent up passion that she had tried so hard to deny.

She had been created for this, she thought wildly when

he eased one strap of her dress down her arm, lower and lower until her small, creamy breast was fully exposed to his gaze. Amazingly she felt neither fear nor revulsion, just a languorous ache deep inside. The feel of his palm against her naked flesh sent a quiver through her and she held her breath when he gently stroked the dusky pink nipple so that it hardened to a throbbing peak.

As she stared at his head, bent low over her breast, she wondered what he would say if she admitted that this was the first time she had allowed any man to touch her so intimately? Undoubtedly he would be shocked, possibly disbelieving. He assumed that the press rumours about her active love life were true and presumably expected her to be sexually experienced.

Only she knew that nothing could be further from the truth.

Damon's breath was warm on her skin and she trembled as he trailed his lips from her collar-bone, down over the soft swell of her breast. With infinite care he stroked his tongue around the darker skin of her aureole, painting moist circles as he edged ever closer to the sensitive tip.

'You don't know how often I've fantasised about doing this,' he murmured before his mouth closed fully around her nipple. Sensation arrowed through her, so intense that it seemed to rip through her entire body, and she arched and clung to him while his words slowly penetrated the sensual haze that enveloped her.

'I want to make love to you, my sweet Annie.'

'Don't!' Her reaction was instant and violent as she jerked out of his arms. 'Don't *ever* call me that.'

'You don't know how often I fantasise about you, Annie— shall I tell you what I'd like to do to you?'

She stumbled to her feet and wrenched the strap of her dress back over her shoulder, so forcefully that her nails left angry weals on her skin. Her stepfather's mocking voice sounded in her head and for a moment it was not Damon sitting on the sofa, but Philip Stone, laughing at her as she struggled to ignore his taunts and get on with her homework.

'My name is *Anna;* do you hear me?'

'I hear, but I sure as hell don't understand,' Damon growled, his bewilderment and frustration clearly visible on his face. 'What's the matter with you? *Theos,* one minute you are warm and willing in my arms, and the next you're a spitting she-cat—with razor sharp claws,' he added slowly when he caught sight of the self-inflicted scratches on her arm. 'Tell me, Anna,' he pleaded huskily, 'what did I do wrong? If I offended you…'

'You didn't…you didn't do anything wrong. It's me—' She broke off and shook her head as the feeling of nausea gradually lessened. 'I'm no good at all this,' she muttered, waving her hand expressively towards the sofa, where minutes before she had responded to his kisses with such fervour.

'You seemed pretty good to me,' he ventured wryly. 'You wanted me, Anna. The desire was not all on one side.' He made a move towards her and then lifted his hands placatingly when she shied away from him. 'Something frightened you,' he said broodingly, 'but I can't help you if you won't confide in me, *pedhaki mou.*'

'I don't need help!' She glared at him, her cheeks burning as she acknowledged that he was probably right. He must believe her to be a head-case. Maybe she was. Her reaction to his lovemaking certainly wasn't normal and yet for a few moments in his arms she had gloried in the pleasurable sensations his caresses evoked.

The strident, repetitive sound of his cell-phone shattered the fragile silence and she frowned when he made no move to answer it.

'Shouldn't you get that?'

'It can wait. This is more important. You and me,' he elaborated grimly, the determination in his eyes filling her with panic.

'There is no you and me. Can't you understand, Damon? I don't want you.' His phone had finally stopped ringing and her voice sounded painfully shrill and over-loud to her ears.

'That's not the message your body was sending out.'

'Well, it's been outvoted. I'm not in the market for casual sex.'

Damon's jaw tightened as he fought to control his anger and Anna quailed at the coldness in his eyes.

'Not from what I've heard,' he commented silkily.

His scathing taunt tore at her already brittle emotions and she couldn't stifle her gasp of distress. His phone rang again but this time she welcomed its intrusion as she forced her arms into her jacket with jerky, uncoordinated movements.

'I have to go,' she muttered numbly.

'Anna…forgive me—that was uncalled for.'

'Forget it.' She clawed back a little of her self-possession and swung away from him. 'And for pity's sake answer your phone and put whoever is so desperate to speak to you out of their misery.'

'We need to talk.' As he spoke Damon snatched up his phone, intent on switching it off, but he glanced at the caller display and hesitated. 'I'm sorry, but I have to take this.'

'I'd like to use the bathroom,' she mumbled.

'Through there,' he indicated the door at the far end of the sitting room, and, without awarding him another glance, Anna hurried across the room.

The door led to his bedroom and she carried on into the *en suite* bathroom where she filled the sink and splashed her face with ice-cold water. Dear God, what was happening to her? She stared into the mirror, looking for answers, but the face looking back at her was ravaged, her eyes full of shadows.

What must Damon think of her? She closed her eyes briefly as if she could somehow shut out her thoughts. She didn't want to think, she just wanted to go home to the safe cocoon of her flat and hide away until she had reassembled her defences.

Her head fell forwards to lean against the mirror and she took several deep breaths in an effort to compose herself before she crossed Damon's bedroom once more. The door leading to the sitting room was slightly ajar and she could hear the deep resonance of his voice as he spoke into his cellphone. He was speaking in his native tongue; she could pick out the odd Greek word and she wondered who had been so eager to talk to him.

From her view of him through the gap in the door, she guessed that the caller was someone with whom he shared a close relationship. His voice was soft and intimate and his body language was relaxed, in stark contrast to the tension that had gripped him a few minutes earlier.

Did he have a mistress back in Greece? she wondered bleakly. Doubtless some dark-eyed, curvaceous beauty who offered uncomplicated sex and wasn't besieged with hangups.

Tears stung her eyes and she blinked fiercely as her gaze fell on the vast king-sized bed that dominated the room. If things had been different, if *she* had been different, would Damon have made love to her on that bed? Would he have peeled her dress from her body, laid her down on the sheets and continued his devastating exploration of every sensitive curve and pulse point?

More than anything she wished that she could be the woman he wanted her to be. Cool, confident Anneliese

Christiansen—style icon and experienced seductress who would match him, caress, for caress, and send him wild with desire. She longed to be a teasing temptress but her stepfather had inflicted irreparable damage to her self-esteem and with it her chance of a normal, loving relationship.

Swallowing the sudden lump in her throat, she peered round the door. Damon was still talking, but any minute now he would finish his call and he had every right to demand an explanation for her behaviour. The thought of a post-mortem was unbearable and she crossed swiftly to the other door that she prayed led straight from his bedroom, out to the main corridor.

Minutes later she stepped out of the lift and hurried over to the reception desk where she requested a taxi. There was no point in prolonging her misery and certainly no point in hoping for some sort of relationship with him when she'd just proved that she was incapable of responding to him like a normal, sexually confident woman.

As she raced down the hotel steps she half expected to turn and see Damon striding across the foyer after her. Only when the taxi sped off through the rain did she finally release her breath. She was unaware that he had arrived downstairs seconds too late and could do nothing but watch her go.

CHAPTER SEVEN

'WHY do you have to go to New York, Papa?'

Damon lifted his gaze from the report that he had been vainly trying to concentrate on for the past half-hour and glanced at his daughter.

Ianthe was sitting on the opposite side of his desk and had covered his once-neat piles of paperwork with her books and a collection of unlikely coloured plastic horses.

'Business, I'm afraid—nothing very exciting.' Which did not explain why his stomach lurched at the thought of the imminent trip, he acknowledged derisively.

The little girl had drawn a picture and was now busy colouring it in. To Damon's technical eye, the pencilled lines of her house were alarmingly crooked but he wisely refrained from pointing it out and watched as she carefully blocked in the roof with a crayon.

'How long will you be away?'

'A week—ten days at the most. Aunt Tina will take care of you as usual.'

There was no pause in the movement of her crayon and he smiled at the sight of her tongue peeping out while she concentrated on keeping the colour within the outline of her drawing.

'Will you be back for my birthday?'

'You think I would miss the most important event of the year?'

Now she looked up and awarded him a grin that spoke of her absolute confidence that he would be there for her special day.

'Remember, I'm going to be nine.'

'I haven't forgotten, *agapetikos*.' Although it seemed hard to believe. His daughter's birth was an event that would be imprinted on his brain for ever. He would never forget his feeling of awe when he had first held her in his arms and looked down at her tiny, screwed-up face.

Eleni had been equally overjoyed at the birth of their first baby—unaware that Ianthe would be her only child. Thankfully they'd had no inkling of the tragedy that would befall ten months later.

Throughout the dark days after Eleni's death, Ianthe had provided his only motivation to get out of bed each day, and now here she was, all pansy-brown eyes and velvet curls, about to celebrate nine years that, despite the loss of her mother, had been filled with happiness.

His daughter was the most important person in his life, Damon acknowledged. Ianthe had no recollection of her mother but she was a confident, well-adjusted child, which was due in no small part to the devotion of his sister. Catalina had willingly stepped in to provide her little niece with a mother figure and even now, despite her marriage and the birth of three children in quick succession, she still treated Ianthe as if she were her own child.

Ianthe finished her artwork and surveyed him solemnly. 'Will you come swimming with me, or are you too busy?' she asked with a theatrical sigh.

Nine years old and already she was adept at winding him around her little finger, Damon thought wryly as he switched off his computer. 'I'm never too busy for you, Ianthe *mou*. Last one in the pool has to swim ten lengths.'

Ianthe sped from the room, squealing with laughter. It was a familiar sound that brought joy to Damon's heart. His daughter laughed a lot and once again he congratulated himself for ensuring that her childhood had not been complicated by a succession of 'aunts'.

He kept his love life strictly separate from his family, fearing that Ianthe might form an attachment to whoever he happened to be dating and be left disappointed when the affair ended. He'd never felt the need to provide her with a stepmother and purposefully avoided telling his various mistresses that he had a child.

Call him a cynic, but he'd learned early on that any mention of the fact that he was a single father encouraged most women in the belief that he must be looking for a replacement wife, when in fact nothing could be further from the truth.

The arrangement worked well and he could see no reason to change it, he brooded as he headed out to the pool. After the disastrous dinner date with Anna, he had returned to Greece determined to forget her. But he was incensed to find that he could not dismiss her from his thoughts. She intrigued him more than any woman he had ever met and, despite her rejection of him, his desire for her was as fierce as ever.

The timing of his business trip to New York was more than a happy coincidence. He was still desperate to discover if the chemistry between them could develop into an affair. But did that necessitate revealing that he had a child?

It was not as if he was planning a long-term relationship with Anna, he reminded himself. He wanted her in his bed, that was all—a series of mutually enjoyable sexual encounters whenever their schedules happened to coincide. But he couldn't forget the visible torment on her face when he had last seen her in London.

She had been pale and tense, her beautiful blue eyes inexplicably full of fear, yet only moments before she had responded to him with a degree of passion that had fuelled his hunger. What the hell had caused her to retreat from him in such panic? And did she respond in similar fashion to the other men she dated, or was he the only man to evoke such an intense reaction?

He didn't even know what he wanted any more, he thought savagely. She'd got him so wound up that he couldn't think straight. With a muttered oath he plunged into the pool and surfaced to find Ianthe bobbing next to him.

'I beat you!' she told him gleefully. 'Never mind, Papa, you'll just have to try harder next time.'

Valuable advice from the mouth of a child, he acknowledged wrily. But as far as Anna was concerned, it was his wisest course of action.

London might be her favourite city in the world, but New York came a close second, Anna decided as she stared out of her hotel window and absorbed the noise and bustle of Times Square. She was a city girl at heart and loved the frenetic pace of the metropolis that never slept.

Since her arrival a week ago, she had lived a punishing schedule of photo shoots and publicity events to mark the twenty-fifth anniversary of the cosmetic house she represented, culminating in last night's lavish party. She'd arrived back at her hotel in the early hours, slept until late and spent an enjoyable afternoon shopping on 5th Avenue.

Not that she needed another pair of shoes, but retail therapy provided her with a much-needed distraction from a certain charismatic Greek who invaded her thoughts with disturbing regularity.

Don't go there, she told herself fiercely and sought to banish the image of Damon's ruggedly handsome face. It had been two weeks since their disastrous date at his London hotel. Two weeks, three days and eighteen hours she amended dismally. She hadn't heard from him in that time and in all honesty could hardly have expected to. Since her hysterical outburst when he'd attempted to make love to her, followed by her ignominious departure, he had doubtless lost all patience with her.

She'd tried telling herself she didn't care. Why on earth would she want an arrogant, overbearing, alpha male in her life? Never mind that he was also a gorgeous Greek demi-god. But she hadn't expected to miss him so much that it was a constant, nagging ache around her heart.

Not that she would cry, she vowed fiercely. Never! And if her face was wet even before she stepped into the shower, it was her secret.

Two hours later her façade of ice-cool elegance gave no sign of her inner turmoil as she stood in the wings, waiting for her cue to step out onto the catwalk. The fashion show was another charity event, sponsored by some of the world's top designers and attended by New York's social élite.

'God, there's not an empty seat out there,' one of the younger models whispered after taking a peep at the packed audience. 'Aren't you nervous? I feel sick.'

'Remember to look straight ahead, not at the audience,' Anna advised with an encouraging smile. Gina couldn't be more than sixteen—it was her first show and she was plainly overawed by the star-studded event. 'That's our cue. Come on—time to go.'

With no visible hint of nerves Anna squared her shoulders and strode onto the runway. As usual the lights blinded her for a few seconds but after eight years on the circuit she knew how to show off the stunning evening gown she was modelling to its best advantage and she walked on confidently. Four more steps, pause for a moment and then turn—the pattern was familiar and afterwards she wondered what had caused her to ignore her own advice and cast her gaze over the audience.

The formidable width of his shoulders and the proud angle of his head were unmistakable and for a brief, stomach-churning second she lost her footing and stumbled. It was only the thought of her utter humiliation should she fall into Damon's lap that enabled her to regain her composure.

Snatching a sharp breath, she tore her startled gaze from his face and swung round to saunter back up the runway. What was he doing here? It must be a coincidence, she reassured herself frantically. It was impossible to believe he had deliberately sought her out after her violent rejection of him the last time they'd met.

From then on the evening became a test of nerve and it was only her professionalism combined with sheer, dogged determination that saw her complete the show.

She refused to glance at Damon again, although every time she neared the end of the catwalk her heart thudded painfully in her chest. But now, as she joined the other models for the finale, her eyes were drawn to him and the ache inside intensified.

He was a playboy and a philanderer—no better than her father. So what madness was it that insisted he was the other half of her soul?

'Hell, I could do with a drink,' one of the other models announced when they fought their way through the backstage chaos. 'Are you staying for the after-show party, Anna?'

Not if she could help it, Anna thought grimly. But her presence at the party was expected and once again her professionalism saw her pin a smile on her face and join the throng of guests.

She noticed Damon the moment she entered the ballroom. In a room full of tall, dominant males, he stood out above the rest. Wealth and power were strong aphrodisiacs and when they were combined with his lethal brand of sexual magnetism it was hardly surprising that he was the subject of intense interest from every female present.

The woman at his side seemed intent on signifying ownership with her hand on his arm and her head tilted slightly so that it was almost resting on his shoulder. God forbid that she should ever appear so desperate, Anna thought scathingly as she fought the corrosive jealousy that burned in her chest. Luisa Mendoza was well-known on the modelling circuit as a man-eater. With her golden skin and mass of luscious black curls she was exquisitely beautiful—an exotic temptress who had obviously wasted no time in hooking her claws into Damon.

She couldn't give a damn whom he dated, Anna told herself impatiently. But the sight of Luisa rubbing herself sensuously, and very unsubtly, against him made her feel sick. At that moment Damon glanced across the room. As his eyes trailed over her she blushed, furious at having been caught staring at him. He held her gaze for a second and then gave a brief nod of recognition before returning his attention to his companion.

He could not have made his lack of interest any plainer and to her horror Anna felt her eyes glaze with tears. She would not break down in public, she told herself fiercely. She longed to return to her hotel but it was her job to chat with the guests who had attended the fashion show and so she gritted her teeth and began to circulate.

The following two hours passed agonisingly slowly but at least she managed to evade Damon and she felt a huge sense of relief when she finally slipped out into the foyer of the fabulous art deco hotel. She had almost reached the main doors when a voice stopped her in her tracks.

'Running away, Anna? You seem to have a habit of sneaking out of hotels.'

'I am not *sneaking* anywhere.'

She swung round, trembling with outrage and fierce awareness when Damon strolled towards her. In his charcoal-coloured suit, grey shirt and burgundy silk tie he was breathtaking. Anna's feet seemed to be rooted to the floor and she swallowed when he halted in front of her, so close that she could almost see the sparks of electricity that arced between them.

'I'm finished here tonight. Duty done. There's no reason for me to stay,' she added pointedly as she allowed her gaze to trawl over him. 'What are you doing here, Damon? Are you interested in fashion?'

'Not in the slightest,' he replied blandly. 'But you know why I'm here, Anna *mou.*' The glint in his eyes warned her that beneath the façade of urbane charm, his hot temper was simmering like volcanic lava waiting to erupt. 'Why did you run out on me in London?'

'My God, you flew all the way across the Atlantic to ask me that? And why now, after no contact for over two weeks?'

'I returned to Greece with the intention of putting you out of my mind,' he admitted grimly.

'From the way you were pawing Luisa Mendoza tonight, you were obviously successful.'

'Unfortunately that intention did not go to plan,' he continued, as if she hadn't spoken. 'And with no disrespect to Miss Mendoza—she was pawing me. I'm not interested in her or any other woman. I have been unable to forget you, Anna—any more than I suspect you've been able to forget me.'

'Did anyone ever tell you that a swollen head is not attractive?' she queried sarcastically, desperate to hide the effect his words were having on her. She tossed her head so that her hair flew around her face in a halo of gold silk. 'What makes you think I've spent the past two weeks pining for you?'

'This,' he said simply before he swooped and captured her mouth in a devastatingly possessive kiss that should have appalled her. Instead it breached her fragile defences so that she could do nothing but stand helplessly in his arms while he continued his flagrant assault of her senses.

His tongue forced entry between her lips to make a skilful exploration, while one hand slid to her nape to angle her head so that he could deepen the caress to a level that was shamelessly erotic. He ran his other hand restlessly over her body, from her waist, over her hip and down to cup her bottom.

Anna gasped when he hauled her close. The unmistakable feel of his arousal pushing against her stomach was new and shocking; yet fiercely exciting as for the first time in her life she became aware of the power of her femininity. There was no doubt that Damon wanted her with a hunger that should have terrified her, but instead of fear she gloried in the irrefutable proof of his desire.

Part of her wanted the kiss never to end and it was only when he lifted his head to stare down at her with a faintly triumphant gleam in his eyes that reality intruded with a vengeance.

'How dare you?' she snapped, her face flaming when she realised that they were incurring curious stares from a number of onlookers. 'If you don't take your hands off me right now, I'll call for Security.'

'Let's spare ourselves such an embarrassing scenario,' Damon drawled, plainly unperturbed by her fury. 'My car's waiting out front.'

'Then I suggest you get in it. I have my own driver, thanks.'

'Not any more—I told him you wouldn't be requiring his services tonight.'

'You've got a bloody cheek!'

Damon was already striding towards the door and Anna hurried after him as fast as her three-inch stiletto heels would allow, determined to give him a piece of her mind.

'There's no need to run. I promise I won't leave without you, *pedhaki mou*,' he mocked gently when she stumbled on the front steps. Before she could think of a suitably blistering retort, he slid his arm around her waist and ushered her over to his limousine.

'This is ridiculous—you can't just kidnap me. I demand that you take me straight to my hotel,' she said in a loud voice intended to alert his driver. The car pulled away from the kerb and she shifted along the seat away from Damon.

'Relax,' he told her idly. 'That's where we're going.'

'But you don't know where I'm staying.'

His slow smile reminded her of a wolf inspecting its prey. Of course he knew where she was staying, she realised shakily. He would have made it his business to find out.

'I can't believe you came all this way just to torment me,' she whispered, unable to keep the faint tremor from her voice.

'I hate to disillusion you but I have a number of important business meetings in New York. When Kezia mentioned that you were here, it seemed a good opportunity to meet up and discover the answer to several pertinent questions—the most important of which, you've already confirmed,' he added with a satisfied smile as his gaze focused on her mouth.

Once again Anna was aware of the sizzling chemistry between them. Raw, primitive, sexual attraction at its most basic, she registered as she felt her nipples harden to tight buds that strained against the soft jersey-silk of her dress. Her frisson of fear was not of what Damon might do, but what she wanted him to do, and she was thankful when the car pulled up outside her hotel.

'I'm sorry to curtail such a fascinating conversation, but it's been a long day,' she said icily. 'There's no need for you to escort me inside.' Her irritation trebled when he slid out of the car and followed her to the door. His amused smile made her want to hit him, her frustration a tangible force as realisation slowly dawned. 'You're staying here, too, aren't you?'

'As a matter of fact, I've been here for the past two days. I'm surprised we didn't bump into each other at breakfast.'

'You really are the most infuriating man I've ever met,' Anna informed him bitterly when he followed her across the reception area and into the lift. *Two days*. He'd been staying here in her hotel for two whole days and hadn't bothered to let her know. It certainly put her in her place, she thought bleakly, unaware that he could decipher every expression that flitted across her face.

'I told you I had urgent business to take care of. But now I'm all yours, *Anna mou*,' he breathed softly. The lift suddenly seemed airless and she inhaled sharply, her eyes locked with his dark velvet gaze.

'You'll forgive me if I don't jump for joy,' she croaked, her attempt at sarcasm lost beneath the huskiness of her tone. The lift halted at her floor and she hurried along the corridor, intent on reaching the sanctuary of her room before he caught up with her. Of course it was hopeless—his long stride easily outmatched hers and she paused outside her door.

'What is it exactly that you want, Damon?'

'Who used to call you Annie? Your father?' he pressed,

when she failed to answer. 'Did he ever hit you, *pedhaki mou?*'

'Of course not.' Anna opened her door and stumbled inside. She was so startled by his question that she didn't register he had followed her into her room until it was too late. 'My father wasn't like that—he was kind and…and funny and I loved him.'

The shimmer of her tears made Damon's gut twist and he had to force himself to continue.

'So who upset you so badly that the mere mention of his nickname for you caused you to react the way you did in London?'

'It doesn't matter. It's none of your business.' Shock, fear, shame—all the emotions her stepfather had once evoked surged through her.

Phil used to accuse her of deliberately leading him on. He'd said it was her fault that he couldn't keep his hands off her and, although common sense told her she had done nothing wrong, there was a part of her that wondered if she had somehow deserved his attention.

Maybe her stepfather was right and she was intrinsically bad. She was an adult now but the fears of an impressionable teenager were still locked inside her head. She would die of shame if Damon ever learned of the things Phil had said to her, the suggestions that even now made her shudder with revulsion. Maybe Damon would believe she had encouraged her stepfather.

With a low cry she spun away from him, her shoulders rigid with tension.

'Go away, Damon. Didn't you get the message when we were in London? I don't want to have anything to do with you.'

'You're lying.'

It wasn't a question but a statement delivered with his usual arrogance.

'My God, what do I have to do to get through to you?' she cried, her eyes wide and despairing when she turned back to face him. 'Leave me alone.'

'How can I when you are inside my head every minute of the day and night?' he growled. 'How can I forget you when you respond to me with such passion? You *feel* it, Anna, the same as I do. There's something between us—chemistry, awareness, call it what you will. All I know is that I have never felt this way about any other woman.'

As he spoke he jerked her into his arms, his dark eyes burning with desire and frustration and a degree of tenderness that made her ache inside. The tears that she had fought to hold back since she had first set eyes on him at the fashion show slid unchecked down her face.

'You don't understand,' she sobbed, beating her hands wildly against his chest.

'Then make me understand.' He ignored the blows she dealt him and tightened his arms inexorably around her until she gave up and crumpled against him, her shoulders heaving. 'I want to have a relationship with you, Anna,' he told her quietly. He tilted her chin and stared down at her. 'Friends, as well as lovers,' he added steadily when she shook her head in fierce negation of the suggestion. 'And I think I understand why you find the issue of trust so difficult.'

She sincerely doubted it, Anna thought grimly. No-one knew the secrets locked inside her head. She had been unable to confide in anyone about her stepfather's unnatural fixation with her and had never spoken about his taunts or the way he had tried to touch her—not even to Kezia.

'Why won't you accept that I'm just not attracted to you?' she muttered as she struggled out of his hold and endeavoured to put some space between them. He seemed to dominate the room and her eyes were drawn to the formidable width of his shoulders and the proud angle of his head. Helplessly she focused on his mouth, remembering the way it had felt on hers, and her lips parted in an unconscious invitation.

'I believe you are as captive to the attraction that burns between us as I am,' he told her seriously. When I hold you—kiss you—your body tells me what you refuse to admit. You want me, Anna, with a passion that matches mine. But events in your childhood—and your father's betrayal in particular—have left you wary of giving in to your emotions.'

'What has Lars got to do with this? I told you, I adored my dad.'

'And he deserted you. He rejected you and chose his second wife's children over you. I understand how devastating that must have been for you, *pedhaki mou*.'

'I doubt it,' Anna muttered wearily. 'My father was a serial adulterer who broke my mother's heart. You can hardly blame me for wanting to avoid the same fate.' She swung away from him, wishing he would just go and leave her in peace. 'I'm tired, and I don't want to talk about it,' she muttered, stiffening when he came up behind her and placed his hands on her shoulders.

'I can't help you until you learn to have some faith in me,' he said gently.

'I don't *need* help, damn it! If ever I do want an analyst, I'll let you know,' she shot back, her attempt at sarcasm lost amid the tears that clogged her throat.

Damon made no reply as he began to massage the tight knot of muscles at the base of her neck. Anna knew she should move, put some space between them, but the feel of his hands on her skin was heaven. He kneaded her flesh with firm, yet gentle expertise, easing her tension so that she gradually felt herself relax.

'Better?' His warm breath feathered her cheek and a soft sigh escaped her. She offered no resistance when he turned her in his arms, her eyes widening a little as she absorbed the warmth in his. Common sense dictated that she should step away from him and demand that he leave. Instead she tilted her head and waited with a curious sense of inevitability for him to capture her mouth in a slow, sensual kiss that demolished her resistance.

This was where she wanted to be, she acknowledged as she wound her arms around his neck. He knew it and there seemed little point in trying to deny it any longer. She knew it was ridiculous, but when Damon held her she felt safe.

She parted her lips, eager to accept the probing warmth of his tongue as he took the kiss to a deeper level of intimacy. Suddenly nothing else mattered—not her father who had destroyed her trust in all men, or her stepfather who had wrecked her self-esteem. All that was important was the feel of Damon's lips on her skin as he trailed a line of kisses along her jaw and found the sensitive pulse point at the base of her throat.

When he lifted his head a fraction she traced her lips over his cheek, paused at the corner of his mouth before initiating a tentative exploration with her tongue. For long moments he allowed her to take control, until his hunger for her became an overwhelming need that saw him slide his fingers into her hair to hold her fast while he took the kiss to a level that was blatantly erotic.

'Damon.' She gave a soft cry when he suddenly swung her into his arms and strode purposefully towards her bedroom. Alarm bells rang faintly in her head but she ignored them. For years her stupid hang-ups had prevented her from exploring her sexuality—but not any more. She wanted Damon to make love to her. She wanted him to release her from her prison of fear and prove that she was a normal, sexually responsive woman.

When he placed her on the bed she clung tightly to him as if she feared that he would withdraw from her.

'Easy, *pedhaki mou*—there's no rush,' he murmured gently when she gripped his shoulders and pulled him down on top of her.

He didn't understand, she thought wildly. She had to do this *now,* while her nerve still held. With a muttered cry she sought his mouth while her fingers scrabbled with his shirt buttons. When she finally freed them she pushed the material aside to run her hands over his chest.

He had an incredible body—lean and powerful, the hard muscles of his abdomen clearly visible beneath his olive-gold skin. His body hair felt slightly abrasive against her palms and she trembled as she imagined how it would feel against the tender flesh of her breasts.

'My turn,' he teased softly as his hand moved to untie the straps of her halter neck. He must be a mind-reader, Anna decided feverishly when he slowly peeled the material down her body to leave her pale breasts exposed to his gaze. She watched the way his eyes darkened, recognised the elemental hunger in his gaze and gave a soft moan when he lowered himself onto her so that they lay together, skin on skin.

His lips trailed a sensual path from her mouth, down her throat to nestle briefly in the valley between her breasts. Anna held her breath when he cupped each soft mound in his palms before he lowered his head to stroke his tongue across one sensitive peak and then the other. Exquisite sensation flooded through her and she slid her fingers into his hair, silently urging him to continue working his magic.

Perhaps understanding her desperation, he drew one nipple fully into his mouth and suckled her until she arched beneath him and rocked her hips against his with devastating effect.

'*Theos,* Anna, I don't think I can wait,' he muttered

hoarsely. He lifted his head for a second, his face a taut mask of desire, before he flicked his tongue over her other tight bud, watching with apparent fascination as it hardened to a throbbing peak that begged for his attention.

Anna closed her eyes and gave herself up to the wondrous sensations Damon was arousing within her. Her body felt as though it were on fire and the dull ache in the pit of her stomach intensified until it was a clamouring need. She shifted her hips restlessly as molten heat pooled between her thighs and even when she felt him tug her dress down, over her hips, she was still utterly certain that this was what she wanted to do.

The brush of his hand on her inner thigh made her quiver with excitement. Her only covering now was a tiny triangle of lace and she inhaled sharply when she felt his fingers dip beneath the waistband to stroke gently through the downy curls at the apex of her thighs.

This was still good, she told herself frantically as the first doubts crept into her head. She was aware of his fingers sliding lower, knew instinctively that any second now he would part her and touch her where she wanted him most.

Oh, God, she wanted him to continue, wanted it desperately, but the heat was draining from her body. Where she had been wet and ready for him, now she was dry, her muscles rigid with tension as the image of her stepfather's leering smile pushed into her mind.

'Shall I tell you where I'd like to touch you, Annie?'

'What is it, Anna *mou?'* Damon lifted his head to smile down at her with tender passion. She stared at him wildly, willing herself to relax, but she couldn't do it. As his fingers gently stroked her she jerked her legs together and pushed her hands against his chest.

'No, *no!* I can't. Please, Damon, let me up. Please,' she whispered, unconsciously pleading for his forgiveness as she watched his face tighten until his skin seemed to be stretched over the sharp angle of his cheekbones. 'I'm sorry. I can't do this. I'm sorry.'

As he rolled away from her she snatched her robe from the end of the bed and thrust her arms into it before dragging it tightly over her breasts. She felt sick. Any minute now she would actually throw up. It would be the final humiliation and she snatched air into her lungs—great, gasping breaths that made her chest heave.

She could hardly bear to look at Damon, sure that she would see both disgust and contempt in his gaze. But when she dared to peep at him, she saw neither. He simply looked weary and curiously deflated. She could almost believe that she had hurt him and the thought made her crumple.

'You must hate me.' She was determined not to cry in front of him but was powerless to prevent the tears that slid down her face. She heard his heavy sigh and crossed her arms over her chest when he stood and walked towards her. He had refastened his shirt buttons in the wrong holes and the mistake was a telling indication of his inner torment that made her tears flow faster.

'Why must I hate you?' he queried gently.

'You must think I'm a tease—that I deliberately led you on and then—' She broke off and shook her head, unable to continue.

'Is that what you were doing, Anna? Were you deliberately taunting me?' His tone was flat and so devoid of any emotion that she had no idea what he was thinking. Did he really despise her? The thought was unbearable and she lifted her head to stare into his eyes.

'No. I wanted you. I thought I could do it. I honestly thought I could go through with it,' she whispered huskily.

It was a peculiar phrase and Damon frowned. She had responded to him with such passion that he had believed she wanted to make love with him. The idea that she had been steeling herself to 'go through with *it*' was repugnant to him. Did she really view him as some sort of ogre? Yet she had seemed so eager when he had first carried her into the bedroom.

He'd known he was rushing her and was furious with himself. He'd planned to take it slow and had come to New York with the intention of wooing her until he won her trust. Instead he'd acted with all the finesse of Neanderthal man. It was little wonder she was staring at him so fearfully, he told himself impatiently.

The naked vulnerability in her eyes made him long to draw her into his arms and hold her close but he restrained himself and reached out to smooth her hair back from her face.

'I don't hate you, Anna—far from it. But I admit, I don't always understand you,' he added ruefully. 'In my eagerness to make love to you, I mistook your response to me as an invitation to take you to bed.

'I fear I am not as patient as your previous lovers,' he groaned, his frustration with himself evident in the darkness of his eyes. 'But I appreciate your need to feel that you can trust me before we take our relationship any further.'

His gentle understanding tore at Anna's fragile emotions. From the first he had been honest about what he wanted from her and it was about time she returned that honesty.

'My previous lovers—who would they be, Damon?'

He shrugged, a faint stain of colour running along his cheekbones. 'Your affairs are headline news, but I'm not criticising you, *pedhaki mou,* I can hardly claim to have lived like a monk myself.' He raked his hand through his hair, unable to disguise his frustration as he struggled to understand her. 'Have your other boyfriends let you down? Is that what this is about?'

'There haven't been any other boyfriends—not in the way you mean,' she whispered, her heart thudding painfully in her chest as she absorbed his stunned expression. 'I've never had a lover.'

'But what of the other men in your life…the numerous love affairs reported in the tabloids?'

'Gossip and speculation by editors desperate to boost sales of their rags,' she explained with a harsh laugh. 'For some reason my photo on the front cover of magazines increases sales, and an article concerning my supposed sex life sells even better. Some of the men I've been linked with are friends, nothing more. Others I've barely met, but they believe that having their name linked with mine will be a good career move. I warned you not to believe every trashy article about me,' she taunted, trying to sound flippant to disguise her hurt

'Are you telling me you're a *virgin?*'

In different circumstances the utter disbelief in his voice would have been comical but Anna had never felt less like laughing.

'It's not a crime, you know.' To her horror she felt her eyes glaze with tears and she swung away from him, desperate to hide her distress. 'I'd like you to leave now. I'm tired and I want to go to bed.' Her eyes fell on the rumpled sheets where a few moments ago she had *ached* with desire for him. Now the ache was around her heart but she would rather die than suffer the humiliation of having him pity her.

'Anna, I…' He reached out to her but she jerked away and fled towards the bathroom.

'Just go, Damon,' she begged brokenly. 'Accept that I am not the woman you thought I was—the experienced seductress you want me to be. I'm sure there must be a dozen blondes in your little black book who can offer uncomplicated sex,' she choked as she scrubbed her wet face with her hand. 'Trust me, you're wasting your time with me.'

CHAPTER EIGHT

WHEN Anna finally found the courage to emerge from the bathroom she was relieved to discover that Damon had gone. She crawled into bed and cried until there were no more tears left, before falling into a restless sleep.

Next morning she woke feeling like death and stumbled into the bathroom to stare at her blotchy face and puffy eyes. She'd read somewhere that crying was supposed to be cathartic, a natural purging of emotions, but all it had done was leave her with a murderous headache.

It took several minutes for her to realise that the knocking sound was coming from the door, rather than someone performing a clog dance inside her head. Muttering a curse, she went to answer it and stared in bemusement at the smiling waiter.

'Room service,' he announced breezily as he steered his trolley past her.

'There must be some mistake. I didn't order anything,' she protested. 'You must have the wrong room.'

'Number 158, breakfast for two,' he insisted. He began to unload the contents of the trolley onto the table. 'We have orange juice, coffee, eggs, hash browns, bagels…'

'All I want is a couple of aspirin and a cup of tea,' she muttered weakly, her stomach churning at the thought of food.

'Yes, you do look a bit rough this morning. It's lucky the editors of *Vogue* magazine can't see you right now,' a familiar accented voice sounded from the doorway. 'That will be all, thanks,' Damon dismissed the waiter and strolled into the room, his lips twitching at the sight of Anna's outraged glare.

'I've spent the night from hell. Is it any wonder I look *a bit rough?*' she demanded furiously. Having believed that she would never have the courage to meet his gaze again, she was now seriously tempted to throw a bagel at his head, followed by the coffee-pot.

She placed her hands on her hips, quivering with rage and another, rather more disturbing emotion when he crossed the room and gently tilted her chin.

'You will always be the most beautiful woman in the world to me, *Anna mou.*'

'Don't.' The inherent tenderness in his tone brought fresh tears to her eyes and her lashes fell.

'I'm sorry you had a bad night. If it's any consolation, mine was possibly worse.'

She lifted her head to study his face and noted the faint lines around his eyes and the deeper grooves on either side of his mouth. Bad night or not, he still looked gorgeous, she thought numbly when his mouth curved into a soft smile that melted the ice around her heart.

'I understand you're free today,' he said cheerfully. Although he did not offer an explanation of how he knew, Anna noted irritably. 'I thought we'd have a lazy breakfast and then spend the rest of the day exploring the city—maybe take a cruise around Manhattan. The full trip takes about three hours and guarantees excellent views of all the famous landmarks.'

'Why?' Anna queried huskily, trying hard not to get caught up in his enthusiasm. Her most sensible course of action would be to catch the next flight home and try to forget she had ever met Damon Kouvaris.

'Why take the boat trip? It seems a more relaxing way of seeing the sights than by road, but there are plenty of bus tours if you'd prefer.'

'That's not what I meant, and you know it. You don't have to spend the day with me. It won't change anything,' she said awkwardly, her cheeks suffusing with colour at his quizzical glance.

'I'm not expecting you to leap into bed with me as payment for an entertaining day out,' he informed her dryly. 'I would simply like to spend some time with you, Anna,' he added softly as he cupped her jaw and lifted her face to his.

His kiss was sweetly evocative, his lips as light as gossamer on hers before he lifted his head to stare into her eyes. 'I don't know what happened in your past, *pedhaki mou,* and, without resorting to thumbscrews, I can't force you to confide in me. Something—someone obviously hurt you so badly that you're afraid to put your trust in anyone. But I'm not simply going to walk away from you.'

'Even knowing that I'll never be able to make love with you?' she whispered. 'Because I can't, Damon. Last night, I thought it would be all right. I wanted you so much,' she admitted with a raw honesty that shook him. 'But when it came to it, I just…froze.' Tears filled her eyes and she blinked furiously. What was it about this man that left her emotions in tatters?

Damon slid his arms around her and she felt him brush his lips against her hairline. 'Never is a long time. Let's just take it one day at a time. You froze last night because I rushed you and you weren't ready. I understand how important trust is to you, Anna. You need to feel confident that I won't hurt you or let you down. All I'm asking for is a chance to prove that you can have faith in me.'

He was impossible to resist, Anna thought weakly as she laid her head on his chest and absorbed his strength. Where she had expected him to be angry with her, or at least impatient, he had shown her nothing but understanding and kindness. It was a long time since she had felt cared for and she feared it could become addictive.

Damon dropped a light kiss on the tip of her nose and led her over to the table. 'I hope you're hungry. This is breakfast New York style,' he smiled as he surveyed the laden table.

'I'm starving,' Anna replied, surprised to find it was true. After a night of utter misery she'd thought she would never be able to eat again, but to her amazement she discovered that her appetite had returned. She sat down and heaped a pile of fluffy scrambled eggs onto her plate. 'Aren't you going to join me?'

Her tentative smile caused a curious pain in Damon's gut. With her face scrubbed free of make-up and her hair caught up in a pony-tail, she looked young and painfully innocent. Although he was still reeling at the thought of just how innocent, he acknowledged grimly.

He didn't doubt for a second that she had spoken the truth when she'd admitted her complete lack of sexual experience. He only wondered how he had missed the signs for so long. He had been guilty of believing all the trash written about her, but her determination to raise money for the children's hospice should have told him she was nothing like her image of a spoilt supermodel.

Anna was beautiful inside and out, but she was also emotionally fragile and haunted by demons from her past. He'd spent a hellish night wrestling with his conscience, knowing that he had neither the time nor the capability to help her. He had commitments she knew nothing about—*baggage* in the form of a child who would always be his first priority.

When *was* a good time to drop into the conversation that you had an eight-year-old daughter? he brooded darkly. The situation had never arisen before. In the years since Eleni's death, he'd never felt the slightest inclination to deepen his relationship with any of his mistresses to the level where Ianthe became an issue.

But Anna was different. He...*cared,* he accepted as he responded to her smile and watched the way her cheeks flushed with pleasure. He didn't understand how, or why, it had happened, he just knew that he wanted her in his life.

Sex was obviously a problem for her, but rather than lessening his desire it only made him want her more. He wanted to help her overcome her fears. He wanted to tutor her and watch her as she experienced sexual pleasure for the first time. She stirred feelings within him that were primitive and deeply possessive and he was prepared to wait for as long as it took until she felt ready to give herself completely to him.

He took his place at the table and helped himself to food, although his appetite had deserted him. How the hell could he ask her to trust him when he was guilty of keeping a fundamental part of his life from her? He had to tell her about Ianthe, and sooner rather than later.

'...Damon.'

He was suddenly aware that Anna was speaking to him and forced himself to focus.

'It's fine if you've changed your mind about today,' she murmured, unable to hide her uncertainty. 'I'm sure you have better things to do than spend the day with me.'

'No,' he replied with simple honesty, 'there's nothing I would rather do than be with you.' He paused for a heartbeat and then added, 'How long do you plan to spend in New York?'

'You mean you haven't already checked my diary?'

Her brows arched in a look that was pure Anneliese Christiansen—ice-cool and disdainful—before her face broke into an impish smile that was the real Anna. 'I have a photo shoot booked for next week, but there's little point in flying home between now and then. Besides, I'm quite happy to have some free time here. How about you?' she queried hesitantly. 'I assume you have to return to Greece soon.'

'I am my own master and I can do whatever I choose,' he told her with a flash of his outrageous arrogance. 'And I choose to stay until next week.' His eyes gleamed with sensual heat as he trapped her gaze. 'So, here we are, two people alone in Manhattan. I suggest we team up for the next few days. Safety in numbers and all that,' he added with a grin.

'Are you saying I'd be safe with you?'

'You have my word, *pedhaki mou*.' His voice lost its teasing edge and he regarded her steadily, noting the betraying tremor of her mouth. 'You can trust me, Anna *mou*.'

Anna had always believed that New York was an amazing city but with Damon it became truly magical. As he had suggested, they boarded a cruise boat at the harbour and enjoyed a leisurely trip around Manhattan, their eyes drawn to the towering skyscrapers that dominated the horizon.

He was an attentive and tactile companion. On the boat he stood behind her and slid his arms around her waist to draw her against the solid strength of his chest. The steady thud of his heart was strangely comforting and although Anna stared determinedly at the view, she was overwhelmed with longing to turn and bury her face in his shirt.

After lunch they took the ferry from Battery Park across to the Statue of Liberty. As they strolled around the base of the great monument he threaded his fingers through hers with an easy familiarity that dismantled her defensive barriers one by one. She didn't understand what he wanted from her—why he was here—but suddenly she no longer cared.

When he paused and drew her into his arms, she stared up at him, silently willing him to cover her mouth with his own. He aroused feelings within her that she'd never experienced with any other man. The knowledge should have terrified her but she was tired of being scared.

Damon had given his word that he wouldn't attempt to rush her into a sexual relationship before she was ready, and she knew with complete certainty that he would never try and force her.

She had never believed she could trust any man but maybe, just maybe, he was different.

As the week slipped past she realised with growing certainty that Damon was unlike any man she had ever met. To the outside world he was a successful, powerful and undoubtedly ruthless businessman at the top of his game. But there was another side to him that she guessed few people outside his immediate family were privileged to meet.

Only a truly confident man could team strength with gentleness and a tender consideration that made her want to weep. Damon had the ability to make her feel like a princess. She adored the way he treated her as if she were infinitely precious to him, even though she knew in her heart that it could not be so.

He could have any woman he wanted. Why on earth was he wasting his time with a sexually inexperienced novice who was incapable of satisfying him?

It was a question that increasingly demanded an answer the more time she spent with him.

'You're very quiet, *pedhaki mou*. Are you tired?'

'A little—but it's been a wonderful day. My head's still buzzing from everything we saw today.' They had spent several hours at the 'Met'—the world famous Metropolitan Museum of Art—and Anna felt as though her senses had overdosed on the visual feast of fantastic exhibits. Tonight they had dined at one of New York's finest restaurants and afterwards Damon had surprised her with a romantic carriage ride through Central Park.

Now they were back at their hotel and he had accepted her invitation to join her for a nightcap in her suite. The natural conclusion to the magical evening they'd spent together was for him to sweep her into his arms and carry her through to the bedroom, where they would spend the night making love.

If she was a *normal* woman, she would saunter over to him, link her arms around his neck and issue him with a bold invitation to take her to bed. But she was not normal, Anna brooded miserably. She was frigid—unable to enjoy or bestow sexual pleasure, even with the man who was fast capturing her heart.

'What is it, Anna? Do you want me to go?'

She was standing by the window, staring unseeingly at the myriad neon lights that lit up Times Square. As Damon spoke he moved to stand behind her and slid his arms around her waist to draw her up against the solid wall of his chest.

'I guess you should…it's getting late,' she whispered, helpless to disguise the tears that clogged her voice. She offered no resistance when he turned her to face him, and watched the way his eyes darkened as he caught the trickle of moisture with his thumb pad. 'I wish things could be different,' she admitted despairingly. 'You've been so kind to me these past few days and I feel I should…'

'Sleep with me? Offer yourself like a sacrificial virgin because I've been *kind* to you? Anna, when you come to me it will be because you want to make love with me, not because you feel obligated,' he assured her.

'But what if that day never comes? How can you be so sure? There must be literally dozens of women willing to fall into your bed,' she muttered, fighting a wave of nausea at the mental image of him holding another woman in his arms.

'I only want you, Anna *mou*. No one else will do. And you are not completely immune to me,' he added softly as his arms tightened around her. 'You simply need time to feel comfortable with me before we can enjoy a fully intimate relationship.'

Comfortable! Dear God, she felt anything but. Comfortable conjured up an image of easy familiarity that was a million miles away from the fierce tension that suddenly gripped her. The sensual heat in Damon's eyes sent fire coursing through her veins and she trembled with anticipation rather than fear when he lowered his head.

He had kissed her several times during the past week—gentle, tender kisses that were bound by the tight restraint he exerted over his emotions. Anna had appreciated his sensitivity. He'd promised not to rush her and was obviously determined to honour that promise, but there was a part of her that had longed for him to lose control and kiss her with the fierce passion she glimpsed in his simmering gaze.

Now that passion was a force he could no longer deny and he claimed her lips with uncompromising hunger. It felt so right, she thought wonderingly as she parted her lips and revelled in the masterful sweep of his tongue. With Damon she didn't feel dirty or ashamed. He brought her to life so that every nerve ending quivered to his touch.

For the first time in her life she relished the feeling that she was a sensual, sensuous creature. Her body seemed to have been created solely for the purpose of giving and receiving pleasure and she exalted in the thrusting proof of his arousal pushing against her stomach.

She followed blindly when he led her over to the sofa and drew her down onto his lap. He captured her mouth again in a slow, seductive kiss that drugged her senses so that she was mindless to everything but the feel of his hands on her body, and she shivered with excitement when he began to unfasten the tiny pearl buttons at the front of her top. She remembered how it had felt when he had caressed her breasts and already her nipples had hardened in anticipation of the pleasure to come.

Damon freed the final button, but to Anna's disappointment he made no move to slide the soft satin from her shoulders. She stirred restlessly in his lap and he groaned and clamped her hips to prevent her from moving.

'I am not made of stone, *pedhaki mou*. If you don't keep still, I'm likely to do something that will shock you and embarrass me.'

She stared at him wordlessly, her cheeks flaming at the erotic images his words evoked. She didn't want him to stop, she acknowledged with a sense of wonderment. She wanted him to kiss her again, touch her where she ached to be touched, and she swayed towards him, her eyes unconsciously pleading.

'I don't think you could shock me,' she told him seriously. 'I feel safe with you, Damon, and I want you to kiss me… touch me,' she admitted huskily.

She felt his chest heave—as if he were a drowning man snatching for air—and she noted that the hand he used to stroke her hair back from her face was not quite steady. His eyes had darkened to the colour of mahogany, lit by a flame of desire that made her tremble with an answering passion.

'You are so beautiful, Anna *mou*. I have never hungered for any woman the way I hunger for you,' he muttered rawly. 'But I won't rush you, or hurt you, and I give you my word that I'll stop the moment you ask me to.'

Maybe she wouldn't want him to stop, Anna thought as he claimed her lips once more in a fierce, hard kiss. Hope surged through her and she opened her mouth to accept the bold sweep of his tongue. She trusted Damon to keep his word, but maybe she would be so caught up in the pleasure he evoked that her fears would remain in the far recess of her mind.

The fine boning of her top provided sufficient support for her small breasts without the need for a bra. She gave a murmur of approval when he pushed the material aside and cupped each pale mound in his big hands. The brush of his thumbs across her swollen nipples sent sensation flooding through her and she moaned softly and allowed her head to fall back so that her breasts were fully exposed to his gaze.

Damon trailed his lips down her throat and continued an inexorable path lower, to stroke his tongue over one tight peak until it throbbed for his full possession. Anna shifted on his lap and slid her hands into his hair to hold him to his task, whimpering when his lips finally closed around her nipple and he suckled her.

By the time he transferred his attention to her other breast she was shaking with a combination of shock that what he was doing to her could feel so good, and a burgeoning need for more. There was nothing in her mind other than a feverish desire for him to assuage the ache that was building inside her and when he slid his hand beneath the hem of her skirt she quivered at the butterfly touch of his fingers skimming the sensitive flesh of her inner thigh.

He paused, mistaking the little gasp she gave as a request for him to cease his gentle exploration of her body. 'Is it too much, Anna? Do you want me to stop?' he whispered, his breath grazing her shoulder as he lifted his head to look into her eyes.

Slowly she shook her head in negation and watched the

smouldering heat in his gaze when she leaned towards him and initiated a tremulous kiss that stirred his soul. For a moment he allowed her to maintain control before he deepened the kiss to another level that was flagrantly erotic. His tongue was an instrument of sensual delight and he explored her with a thoroughness that left his desire for her in no doubt.

Anna was aware of his hand sliding higher and higher beneath her skirt but the pressure of his mouth on hers was creating such havoc with her emotions that she felt neither fear nor revulsion when he gently stroked his fingers over the tiny triangle of lace at the junction of her thighs. Desire flooded her, leaving her hot and slick, and she held her breath when he eased his fingers beneath her knickers to initiate an intimate exploration that was new and utterly beautiful.

She parted for him like a rose opening its velvety petals to the sun and with infinite care he slid in deep, feeling her muscles spasm around his finger. She was tighter than he had expected and he was desperate not to cause her pain, but rather than wanting him to withdraw she seemed intent on urging him to continue caressing her.

Anna closed her eyes; her whole body focused on the incredible sensations Damon was arousing. Her body felt on fire, with the brightest flame burning at her central core. She wasn't even sure what she wanted, just knew that it was there, hovering, and with a little cry of frustration she rocked her hips and pushed herself against his hand.

Damon seemed to sense the tumultuous sensations that were building inside her and began to move his finger with little pulsing strokes. At the same time he rubbed the tip of his thumb over the acutely sensitive nub of her clitoris, and Anna's world exploded.

Spasm after spasm ripped through her so that she

trembled in his arms. It was frighteningly new and yet so utterly exquisite that she wasn't afraid. She threw her head back and cried out; unaware of the pleasure he took from watching her climax for the very first time.

An emotion that was deeply primitive surged through Damon. Anna was his woman and his alone. No other man had ever caressed her so intimately or made her cry out with the pleasure of sexual release.

She was his and he would treasure her always, he vowed as he felt her tremors gradually lessen. Whatever had happened in her past still haunted her. There was still some way to go before she would feel confident enough to give herself to him completely. But he could wait, God help him. He would use his iron will-power to control the desire that threatened to overwhelm him and one day his patience would be rewarded and he would be able to penetrate her fully so that their bodies were joined as one.

The thought was enough to make his penis strain uncomfortably against the restriction of his trousers and with one swift movement he stood with her still in his arms. The pressure of her pert bottom rubbing against him was enough to tempt a saint but he had promised not to rush her and he would keep that promise, even though he would probably spend the rest of the night beneath a cold shower.

Anna opened her eyes as the room swayed alarmingly, and discovered that Damon was carrying her purposefully towards her bedroom. He had given her more pleasure than she had believed it was possible to experience. Even now, little quivers of aftershock were spiralling through her. It was only fair that he should want to experience the same sexual ecstasy, she told herself as she tried to ignore her frisson of apprehension.

When he placed her on the bed, she stared at him silently, unaware of the stark vulnerability in her eyes when she gave him a tremulous smile. He would be gentle; she knew it. She trusted him. He wasn't a barbarian and he certainly wasn't the balding, sweaty, middle-aged excuse for a man that her stepfather had been.

Damon would never mock her or make her feel tainted, she frantically reminded herself. But as he leaned over her she felt her breath catch in her throat so that her chest jerked unevenly.

'I'll give you some privacy to get undressed,' he said in a matter-of-fact tone that brought her crashing back to reality.

She blinked at him in bemusement when he gathered up her nightshirt and handed it to her and his next sentence added to her confusion.

'Can I get you something—a cup of tea perhaps?'

Tea! He wanted to calmly sit and drink tea as if they were at a vicarage tea party before he threw her down on the bed and made passionate love to her. If she hadn't been terrified out of her wits at the thought of the passionate lovemaking, Anna would have found the situation hysterical.

'I'm fine, thanks,' she croaked, clutching her nightshirt in front of her naked breasts like a talisman. Damon gave her a brief smile before he strolled into the sitting room and it was only when he had closed the door between them that she released her breath.

She had no idea how long her reprieve would last and shot into the bathroom where she scrambled out of her skirt and into the nightshirt, washed her face and brushed her teeth, all in record time.

She could do this, she told her reflection, desperately trying to ignore the fact that every last vestige of desire that Damon had aroused in her earlier had disappeared. Her nerves were at screaming point, and the sensual heat that had flooded between her thighs had gone, leaving her as dry and barren as a desert. But she could do this.

For a second, her stepfather's face leered back at her and she blinked hard to dispel his image from her mind. She heard faint sounds from the bedroom. Damon was waiting for her and sick fear lurched in the pit of her stomach. She couldn't remain a virgin for the rest of her life. Better to get the first time over with. And at least she trusted him enough to know he would be patient.

She looked like a small lamb at the gates of the slaughterhouse, Damon thought grimly when Anna emerged from the bathroom. Her voluminous white cotton nightshirt, decorated with yellow daisies, was curiously childlike and he wanted to draw her into his arms and simply hold her close. Instead he turned back the bed sheets with brisk efficiency and patted the mattress.

'Come on, in you get. You look all in, *pedhaki mou.*'

Fighting the urge to flee from the room, Anna obediently climbed into bed and lay down. Damon was still fully clothed. Perhaps he intended to strip in front of her, she speculated frantically, and squeezed her eyes shut to block out the image of him peeling the clothes from his body.

She felt him draw the covers over her and when the mattress dipped she dared to peep between her lashes to discover him sitting, still clothed, on the edge of the bed.

'I thought we could try and get tickets for a Broadway show tomorrow—if you'd like to?'

'That sounds…nice,' she muttered stiffly, finding it hard to make plans for the next day when there was still the night to get through.

Damon stood up but made no effort to remove his clothes. 'Good. I'll make enquiries at Reception in the morning. Sleep well, Anna.' He leaned over and brushed his lips over hers in a gentle benediction before he strolled across to the door.

'But I thought…' She jerked upright and stared at him in

bewilderment. 'I assumed you were going to stay the night.' Faced with his silence, she chewed on her bottom lip, her cheeks scarlet as she ploughed on. 'Earlier, when we...when I—' oh, God, this was difficult '—I didn't satisfy you.'

'On the contrary, Anna *mou,* the fact that I was able to give you pleasure gave me more joy than I've ever known,' he told her gravely. 'Soon I hope to make love to you fully, but only when you're ready—only when you trust me enough to give yourself to me without fear or reservation.

'Until then I will sleep in my own bed, although it may be necessary to spend most of the night beneath a very cold shower,' he admitted with a wry smile that tugged at her heart.

'Sweet dreams, Anna. I'll see you at breakfast,' he bade her softly, before he stepped out of her room and closed the door behind him.

CHAPTER NINE

ANNA slept fitfully and woke at dawn to spend the next couple of hours rehearsing what she wanted to say to Damon. After showering, she blow-dried her hair so that it fell in a sleek gold veil around her shoulders before selecting white linen trousers and a lacy top from the wardrobe. The finished effect was cool and elegant, and hopefully masked the fact that inside she was a seething mass of emotions.

At eight she could wait no longer and took the lift to his floor, her heart hammering in her chest when she headed down the corridor to his suite. The patience and understanding he'd shown the previous night had proved irrefutably that she could trust him. She accepted that they would never have a proper relationship until she told him about her stepfather and now she was ready to confide in him.

Perhaps Damon would be able to dismiss the fears that Philip Stone had put into her head—the idea that sex was grubby and disgusting. Common sense told her that making love was a perfectly natural act but she needed Damon's strength and sensitivity to convince her.

'I know it's early, but I couldn't wait to see you,' she said shyly when he answered his door. 'I thought we could have breakfast together…' She tailed to a halt and stared at his grim face.

He looked terrible. His face was haggard, with deep lines etched around his mouth. His grey suit was impeccably tailored but he'd obviously not found time to shave, and his jaw was shaded with black stubble.

'Damon, what's wrong?'

'I have to go home. Today. Now.' His accent was very pronounced—an indication of his stress levels—and as he strode across to his bedroom he spoke into the cell phone clamped to his ear, in terse, voluble Greek.

'I'm sorry, Anna,' he said when he finished the call and turned to find her hovering uncertainly in the doorway. 'It's an emergency. I can't get on a damn flight for hours, so I've chartered a private jet.' As he spoke he bundled several bespoke, Egyptian cotton shirts into his case with as much care as if they were rags, before drawing the zip shut. With a final glance around the room, he snatched up his jacket and headed for the door, frowning when she continued to block his path.

'I'll call you,' he promised distractedly, but it was only when she put her hand on his arm that he seemed to really register her presence.

'What's happened? What sort of emergency? Please— don't shut me out, Damon,' she pleaded. 'Maybe I can help?'

He took a deep breath, as if he had to force himself to be patient with her. 'There's been an accident back in Greece. Everything's under control and there's nothing you can do. I just need to get home as quickly as possible.'

'But who…a member of your family—why is it such a secret?' Anna broke off, appalled by the thought that had suddenly struck her. 'Do you have a mistress in Greece? Is that why you won't tell me?'

'*Theos,* why do you always think the worst?' he growled savagely. 'I don't have a mistress—in Greece or anywhere else.'

'Then who has been hurt in an accident?' she demanded. 'I thought we were friends, Damon—that there was something between us. Surely you can tell me?'

For a moment he looked as if he would ignore her. His face was a tight mask, his eyes shadowed and unfathomable, but then he turned—his hand already on the door handle— and stared at her.

'My daughter has fallen off her bike and is in hospital with concussion. Tests have detected a slight swelling on the brain. That's why I have to go.'

The silence in the room vibrated with tension as Anna struggled to assimilate his words. He had to be making some sort of cruel joke, she decided numbly. This was Damon, the man whom, during the long hours of the night, she had decided that she could trust with her life. How could he have a child and not have told her?

'Your daughter?' she said thickly, desperately trying to moisten her parched lips. 'You have a daughter? But when…how?' She shook her head. 'I don't understand.'

'It's quite simple,' he said brusquely. The look of shocked disbelief in her eyes made his gut twist, but there was no time to break the news gently when his adored little girl was lying injured in a hospital bed. 'My wife gave birth to our daughter, Ianthe, ten months before her death.'

'So she…your daughter, she's eight years old?'

'Nearly nine—' He broke off and raked a hand through his hair. 'Look, I realise it must have come as a shock, but I really don't have time to talk about it—her—now.' He pulled open the door, his big body taut with impatience and the need for action. 'I'll call you, *pedhaki mou.*'

'Don't!' Anna gave a harsh laugh. 'Don't call me that. In fact, don't call me at all. I never want to hear from you again, Damon.'

'Don't be ridiculous.' On the point of striding out of the

room, he halted and swung back to stare at her ashen face. 'We need to talk, Anna,' he added more gently when she lifted her bewildered, pain-filled eyes to him. 'But right now my first priority is Ianthe. You must see that.'

· Anna stared at him as if she were truly seeing him for the first time and the contempt in her eyes drove a knife through his heart. 'She should always be your first priority, Damon. My God! She's an eight-year-old, motherless child and you left her alone in Greece while you flew to the other side of the world to try and persuade me into your bed. What kind of a father does that make you?'

'I did not leave her alone,' he snapped furiously, outraged that she should question his abilities as a parent. 'Ianthe has always spent a great deal of time with my sister and her family. She regards Catalina as a surrogate mother and is as close to her cousins as if they were her own brothers.'

'It's not the same,' Anna told him fiercely. 'You are her father, her only parent, and you left her to be with me. I *know* how it feels to be abandoned. To be overlooked in favour of another woman. You're just the same as my father and I can't *believe* I was so stupid as to have actually started to trust you.'

'When have I ever given you cause to doubt my word?' Damon demanded, his eyes smouldering with angry fire.

'You have a child!' Anna yelled at him. 'A child you've never seen fit to mention despite the fact that you urged me to trust you. Why didn't you tell me?' she whispered brokenly, her anger draining away as the enormity of his deception hit her.

Damon looked as though he had been sculpted from marble, his skin stretched taut over the sharp contours of his face. Suddenly he seemed frighteningly distant and remote and she realised with a sickening lurch that she really didn't know him at all. 'In the general scheme of things, I'm not important to you, am I, Damon?'

'At first, no, you were not,' he admitted bluntly. 'I have always kept my private life separate from Ianthe. It's amazing how many women view a multimillionaire single father as prime husband material. And I was not looking for a wife.'

'Are you saying you didn't tell me about your daughter because you feared I would use her as a means to engineer a permanent place in your life? My God, your arrogance is beyond belief.'

Anna fought the wave of nausea that swept over her. Her heart felt as though it had been rent in two but she wouldn't give him the satisfaction of seeing how much he had hurt her. 'You know my feelings on the whole step-parent issue.'

'Which is precisely why I couldn't find the courage to broach the subject,' Damon replied quietly. 'I have known for some time that you are different to my previous mistresses.'

'Yes, I've got a major hang-up about sex. I don't imagine it's a problem that your numerous exes have ever suffered from,' she flung at him bitterly.

'I meant that I...feel differently about you. You mean more to me than any other woman has done since Eleni died,' he admitted slowly.

Incredibly for Damon Kouvaris, he seemed awkward and unsure of himself—a first, surely, for Mr Confidence, Anna thought darkly. The tide of colour that stained his cheekbones was all the more endearing because it was in such contrast to his usual arrogance.

But his embarrassment was probably caused by guilt that he had been caught out, she told herself fiercely as she hardened her heart against him. All the time he had been urging her to trust him, he had been deliberately deceiving her. He was no better than every other man she'd met. No better than her father.

It belatedly occurred to her that somewhere on the other side of the world a frightened little girl was lying alone in hospital with possibly life-threatening injuries. Now was not the time for bitter recriminations. Damon's daughter needed him and the most important thing right now was for him to be by her side.

'Just…go, Damon. Go home to your little girl. Trust me,' she whispered thickly, 'the only person she wants at the moment is her daddy. No one else will do.'

Damon nodded, his face darkening when he moved jerkily towards her and saw her flinch. The silent plea in his eyes tore at Anna's heart but her composure was held together by the most fragile of threads and she knew that if he touched her, it would snap.

She watched as he stepped into the lift, her gaze locked with his until the doors silently closed between them. And then he was gone. Stifling a sob, she hurried back to her room and bolted the door before she gave in to the maelstrom of emotions that hit her with the force of a tornado.

Athens in August was as hot as Hades. During the short walk across the airport car park, Anna had felt the intense heat of the sun on her skin and was glad to climb into the cool interior of the air-conditioned limousine that was waiting to collect her.

The roads leading from the airport were teeming with traffic. The chauffeur seemed unconcerned by the cacophony of hooting from impatient taxi drivers but Anna held her breath when one of the literally hundreds of motorcyclists on the road veered in front of them.

'Have you visited Athens before?' enquired the young woman who was sitting beside her in the back of the car.

'I've worked here a few times but I've never really explored Athens properly, and fortunately I've never had to drive on its roads,' Anna replied dryly. 'Is the studio far from here?'

'We're actually going to my private villa, which is about twenty minutes out of town. I have a workshop and design studio there and I think it will be an ideal place for the photo shoot,' the woman explained, her Greek accent not detracting from the fact that she spoke excellent English. 'I've booked Fabien Valoise. I know you've worked with him before and I was very impressed with the pictures he took of you.'

Anna's brows rose. Tina Theopoulis was obviously sparing no expense in the marketing of her range of exclusive, hand-crafted jewellery. Fabien Valoise was one of the best photographers around and she knew that his diary was booked up for months in advance.

When her agent had first contacted her with details of the assignment in Greece, she had turned it down flat, stating with complete honesty that she would rather fly to the moon than travel to Athens. But Tina Theopoulis—or her financial backers—had been adamant that Anna's cool, Nordic beauty would provide a perfect backdrop for the Aphrodite collection.

It was not the eye-opening financial incentive offered that had finally made her decide to take the job, Anna acknowledged as she stared out at the busy streets. She had no interest in money or her career—no interest in life itself.

For the past month—ever since she had returned from New York—she'd felt as though she were slowly dying inside. She couldn't sleep, and certainly couldn't eat. It was unheard of for a model to be too thin, but her clothes were hanging off her and her eyes looked too big for her gaunt face. She could only hope Fabien Valoise would work his magic with the camera and transform the dull-eyed stick insect she had become into the iconic Anneliese Christiansen that Tina Theopoulis was expecting.

The only reason she had come to Athens was because Damon was here, and, although she hated to admit it, she'd been unable to resist the opportunity to be near him. Not that she expected to actually see him, she conceded miserably. Athens was a big and overcrowded city and the chances of bumping into him were practically zero. But this was Damon's home and her bruised heart took some comfort from knowing that he was near.

The car eventually reached the outskirts of the city and headed out towards the Olympic Village before the road climbed into the mountains.

'Here we are,' Tina murmured when they turned into a driveway and halted in front of a white-walled villa.

'Goodness, what a spectacular place,' Anna commented, her unhappiness momentarily forgotten as she stared up at the villa. 'It's huge, and absolutely beautiful. How many storeys are there—five?'

'Six counting the basement, and there's underground parking beneath that,' Tina replied with a smile. 'We're on the slopes of Mount Parnitha, hence the wonderful view. On a clear day it's even possible to see the island of Aegina.'

'Do you live here alone?' Anna asked curiously when she followed her hostess up the front steps and into a vast, marble-floored entrance hall. Before Tina could reply, three small boys hurtled into the lobby. The oldest couldn't be more than five years old, Anna guessed, while the youngest was little more than a baby, with chubby limbs and an adorable smile.

'Hardly alone, as you can see,' Tina laughed, 'although I sometimes think I would be more productive in my work if I did not have the children.'

'But you wouldn't be without them,' Anna guessed, feeling an unexpected pang of longing when she watched Tina lift the youngest child into her arms. She'd never given much thought to having a family of her own. It was something she'd vaguely imagined for her future—and would only be possible if she ever overcame the seemingly insurmountable problem of trusting a man enough to have a physical relationship with him.

For a brief time she'd believed she could trust Damon, she thought bitterly. But even if by some miracle they met again and embarked on an affair—that was all it would be. Damon had a child who was, rightly, the main priority in his life, and he'd made it clear that he wasn't looking for a permanent relationship with any woman.

'The villa is arranged as two separate residences,' Tina explained as she ushered Anna over to the lift. 'My husband, Kosta, and I live with the boys in the lower rooms and my bro…' she paused, suddenly flustered and pink cheeked, before quickly adding '…and other family members occupy the top floors. My workshop is in the basement. If you'd like to go down, I'll take the children to their nanny and join you in a few minutes.'

The three boys were running boisterously around the lobby. Tina certainly had her hands full, Anna noted when an older child—a girl—suddenly peered over the banister of the ornate central staircase. Four children and a successful career as a jewellery designer—it was an enviable lifestyle, she mused when Tina spoke in Greek to her daughter.

The girl was a few years older than her brothers, with the same dark eyes and black silky curls. She was exceptionally pretty but seemed shy compared to the bold little boys and stared at Anna curiously for a few seconds, before darting off up the stairs again.

'The lift will take you down to the basement where Fabien is already waiting,' Tina murmured, seeming curiously tense. Perhaps she was anxious to make a start, Anna decided as she stepped into the lift. The photo shoot must be costing a fortune and, for a small business such as Theopoulis Jewellery Design, time was money.

As Tina had promised, Fabien Valoise had already arrived. With the help of his lighting engineer, he had turned the design room into a photographic studio and was waiting with the make-up artist, hairdresser and stylist.

'Anna! It's good to see you, *chérie*. How are you?' Fabien greeted her warmly.

Anna dredged up a smile for the thin, angular man, dressed from head to toe in black. She'd worked with him several times in the past and they had become good friends. 'Fabien—it's good to see you, too. I'm fine.'

'Something tells me you're lying, *ma petite*.' Fabien cast a professional eye over her before strolling across the room to greet her with a kiss on both cheeks. 'You've lost weight since I last worked with you. Are you ill, or in love?'

'Isn't one the cause of the other?' Anna queried bitterly. 'Perhaps I'm suffering from a sickness of the heart.'

'Ah! Do you want to talk about it, or do you simply need a shoulder to cry on?' the Frenchman asked with gentle sympathy.

'Neither—I can deal with it,' Anna replied. 'Shall we get to work?'

'Just a couple more shots, *chérie*. Look to the left and lift your chin a little more. Perfect—now look straight at the camera…'

Anna followed Fabien's instructions and moved her head obediently. They had been working for several hours and the hot studio lights had made her feel thirsty, but she knew Fabien hated interruptions and so she ignored the prickling dryness of her throat.

Tina Theopoulis was clearly a gifted artist and jeweller. Anna was impressed with every piece she had modelled, but the wedding collection—comprising a white gold and diamond necklace and drop earrings—was simply exquisite. Diamonds as beautiful as these were almost worth risking marriage for, she thought cynically as she glanced down at the floor-length, oyster silk dress the stylist had chosen for her to wear with the jewellery.

'Okay, *chérie,* we'll take a break,' Fabien murmured.

Anna gave a sigh of relief and stretched her aching muscles, but as she lifted her head her attention was caught by a figure standing at the back of the room. Her heart rate accelerated and she felt sick and dizzy. She must be seeing things! It could not possibly be Damon—was her last conscious thought before the walls closed in and she slid into oblivion.

She opened her eyes to find that her face was pressed against a solid wall of muscle.

'Damon?' she whispered, when a furtive peep upwards revealed a square jaw and the chiselled facial bone structure of a sculpted masterpiece.

He speared her with a brief, furious glance. 'Who else were you expecting?' he demanded curtly.

'Certainly not you—you're the last person I expected or wanted to see. Where are you taking me?' she added sharply as she slowly became aware of her surroundings. At that moment the lift halted and the doors opened into an enormous marble-floored room with huge windows on three sides, which allowed sunlight to pour in.

Damon strode across the room, ignoring her attempts to wriggle out of his arms.

'Will you put me down? You have no right to…to manhandle me,' she cried, her breath leaving her body on a sharp gasp when he dropped her unceremoniously onto one of the wide sofas, scattered with brightly coloured cushions, that were grouped beneath the main window.

Instantly she struggled to sit up, her cheeks the same shade of scarlet as the sofa. 'How dare you interrupt my photo shoot? I'm supposed to be working for Tina Theopoulis—whatever will she think? And what are you doing here? Did you know I would be here?'

'Of course I knew. It's taken me two weeks of constantly badgering your agent to arrange the shoot,' he growled.

He loomed over her, big and powerful and so utterly gorgeous that Anna's heart contracted and she felt the familiar sting of tears. Damn him! For a woman who'd once vowed never to cry over a man, she had shed an ocean over him and she hated herself for her weakness.

Nothing horrified her more than the idea that she was turning into the woman her mother had once been—wasting her life and her emotions on a man who didn't deserve them. But she'd missed Damon so much this past month that every day without him had been more agonising than the last. How could she have let it happen? she wondered as she edged off the sofa. How could she have been stupid enough to fall in love with him?

That last thought was so terrifying that she jumped up, only to have him haul her back down onto his lap and imprison her with arms of steel.

'What did you mean when you said you arranged the photo shoot?' she demanded, hastily dragging her eyes from his face. He was too close for comfort. She could feel the warmth emanating from him and the familiar tang of his cologne set her senses alight. 'Are you Tina Theopoulis's financial backer?'

'Yes, but I'm also her brother. Catalina, or Tina as she is sometimes known, is incredibly talented—don't you think?' He absorbed her look of stunned comprehension and gave a wolfish smile, his eyes gleaming with the familiar heated desire that made Anna tremble. 'Diamonds suit you, *pedhaki mou*,' he murmured softly, sliding his fingers over the ornate necklace at her throat before tipping her head back to claim her mouth in a brief, hard kiss that drove her to the edge of sanity.

Common sense told her she should resist him, but, as was usual when she was in Damon's arms, her brain seemed to lose all power of rational thought and she became a wanton creature, desperately seeking the pleasure his mouth evoked.

Sensing her capitulation, he deepened the kiss until it became a sensual feast that demolished her mental barriers and had her clinging to him, her lips parting helplessly beneath the demanding sweep of his tongue. Finally he lifted his head and stared down at her swollen lips, noting the expression of stunned despair in her eyes. There was still a hell of a way to go, he accepted grimly. But at least she was here, in his arms, and this time he was determined not to let her go.

'Why did you go to such lengths to bring me here?' Anna croaked. She tried to ease off his lap, needing to put some space between her and the temptation he aroused to fasten her mouth on his and lose herself in the exquisite ecstasy of his kiss.

She quickly discovered that her attempts to escape him were futile when he clamped his hands around her like a vice and forced her to remain balanced on his thighs.

'I want some answers—and, as you refused to take any of my calls, kidnapping you was my only alternative,' he told her bluntly.

'Kidnap! You can't possibly believe you can keep me here against my will…' She tailed to a halt, the look in his dark eyes warning her that he intended to do just that. 'My agent will wonder where I am if I don't contact her.'

'I told her to clear your diary for the next month.'

'You've got a damn nerve. This is my career we're talking about.'

'No, our future relationship is the only subject up for discussion,' he said mildly, earning himself a look of such wrath that he had to hide his smile. Angry was good—at least she looked more alive than the pale waif who had looked as though she would snap in the slightest breeze.

'I did answer your first call,' Anna snapped. 'I was glad to hear that your daughter's head injury was not as serious as first believed and that she was recovering well from her bike accident.' She inhaled sharply as a thought struck her. 'The little girl downstairs— that was Ianthe, wasn't it?'

'She's been very excited about your visit ever since I told her about you and she couldn't resist taking a peep,' Damon explained. 'She thinks you look like a princess.'

'But why did you tell her about me? I don't understand what game you're playing, Damon, but it's a dangerous one,' Anna warned. 'I told you the last time we spoke that I won't be drawn into a relationship with you now that I know about your daughter.

'I don't want to be responsible for hurting her like I was hurt when my father walked out,' she added painfully. 'Ianthe is a little girl who needs your full attention and commitment. You have to be there for her and make sure she knows how much you love her. You have to protect her,' she told him fiercely, 'and you can't do that if you're constantly flitting between London and Athens, trying to maintain a long distance affair with me.'

She wiped her hand over her face and was startled to find that her cheeks were wet. Damon had stilled—she could feel the tension in him as he tilted her chin and forced her to meet his gaze.

'Ianthe is in no doubt of my love for her. I would gladly give my life for my daughter. But your father didn't protect you, did he, Anna? That's what all this is about.'

'I don't know what you mean,' Anna lied thickly. She

tried to pull away from him but he cupped her face in his big hand and gently wiped away her tears.

'I spoke to your mother about you.'

'You did *what?*' Anna's eyes flew open. 'How dare you harass members of my family—how did you even know where to find her?'

'It was relatively simple for my private detective to discover that she's living in France with her third husband,' Damon revealed steadily. 'You've never met Charles Aldridge, have you? Your mother couldn't hide her disappointment that you've never visited.' He paused for a moment and then added, 'He seems to be a decent man.'

'Good,' Anna muttered, remembering the promises she'd made to visit her mother's French home, and the last-minute excuses that had prevented her from going.

'A far better choice than her second husband,' Damon said softly. He didn't know what sort of reaction to expect and was unprepared for Anna's violent struggle as she scrambled out of his lap. The patent distress in her navy-blue eyes told him what he already suspected. He knew now who had called her Annie, but for both their sakes he had to make her face her demons.

'Did you know that Philip Stone served a jail sentence for downloading illicit images of young girls onto his computer? I guessed not,' Damon murmured when Anna silently shook her head. 'Your mother left him after he was arrested and immediately started divorce proceedings. She explained that you had already left home by then and, because she didn't want to upset you, she never told you the truth about him. But you knew what he was like, didn't you, *pedhaki mou?* And that was the reason you chose to struggle to live independently at such a young age, rather than return home.'

She was silent for so long that he thought she wouldn't answer, but suddenly she lifted her head. The utter desolation in her eyes made his heart clench and he longed to draw her into his arms, but he knew she would reject him.

'He used to watch me,' she whispered, 'all the time; whatever I was doing in the house, he'd be there, staring at me. At first I thought I was imagining it. I only saw him when I came home from boarding school and I thought maybe I was just being silly.'

She took a deep breath and forced herself to continue. 'But then he started saying things, making personal comments about how my body was developing. I didn't like it, of course—it was embarrassing—but he only did it when we were alone and when Mum was there he was always just normal and friendly.'

'Is that why you didn't say anything to your mother?' Damon asked gently.

'I knew Phil would laugh it off or make out that I was over-imaginative. And Mum was happy. For the first time since my father had left us I actually saw her laughing, after years of watching her crying all the time. I couldn't destroy that happiness,' Anna told him fiercely. 'I would have done anything to see her smile, and my stepfather knew it.

'That was when he started trying to touch me,' she revealed, her face twisting with revulsion as long-buried memories resurfaced. 'He didn't sexually abuse me in the full sense, but he used to brush against me as if by accident and he delighted in telling me, in grotesque detail, exactly what he'd like to do to me.'

'Where was your real father while all this was going on?' Damon queried tightly, fighting to disguise the anger in his voice that anyone could have treated a vulnerable young girl on the brink of womanhood so appallingly.

'He was busy with his new wife and family,' Anna replied quietly. 'I barely had any contact with him and I was afraid he would accuse me of trying to stir up trouble to gain his attention.'

'So the man you should have been able to depend on most failed to protect you,' Damon murmured, quietly. Suddenly everything made sense. Her father had abandoned her and hadn't been there when she'd desperately needed him. She had been forced to cope alone with her stepfather's foul sexual advances. It was little wonder that she was afraid to trust any man.

Despite the late-evening sunshine spilling into the room, Anna was cold and she wrapped her arms defensively around her body as if to prevent herself from falling apart. This was the first time in her life that she had ever spoken about the trauma she'd suffered at the hands of her stepfather. It was as if the floodgates had opened and the words spilled out of her. 'Philip made me feel dirty,' she admitted huskily. 'He made me believe that sex was disgusting, and, although the sensible part of me knows that can't be true, I still hear his voice in my head.

'When you touch me, try to make love to me, I imagine his hands on my body and I can't bear the knowledge that he's out there somewhere, thinking all those disgusting things about me.'

'But he's not, *pedhaki mou.*' Damon stood and swiftly crossed the room to pull her into his arms. Instantly she stiffened but he held her against the broad strength of his chest and stroked his hand through her hair. 'Philip Stone was killed in a car accident two years ago. Whatever happened in the past is over and he can never hurt you again.'

CHAPTER TEN

'ANNA, are you awake?'

Anna opened her eyes and frowned at the sound of the disembodied voice—before she remembered where she was. 'It's all right, Ianthe, you can come in,' she murmured, smiling sleepily when her bedroom door was cautiously pushed open.

'Papa said I wasn't to wake you,' Damon's daughter admitted anxiously, in the fluent English that she spoke as easily as Greek, 'but we're going to Poros today and I can't wait!'

The little girl flung herself on the bed, her riotous mass of black curls dancing on her shoulders and her dark eyes sparkling with excitement. 'It's going to be great. We're going on Papa's boat and when we get to the island we can go swimming in the sea. You will come swimming with me, won't you?'

'Of course,' Anna promised. Ianthe's enthusiasm was impossible to resist. 'I'm all packed. I'll have a quick shower and then I'll be ready. What's the time?'

'Almost nine o'clock,' Ianthe informed her. 'I wanted to wake you earlier, but Papa said you were tired because sometimes you have bad dreams.' She hopped off the bed and followed Anna into the *en suite* bathroom. 'I used to have bad dreams about a monster, but Papa told me not to be scared because he would chase all the monsters away. Do you dream about monsters, Anna?'

Anna stared at her reflection in the mirror and realised that her eyes were no longer full of shadows. 'I used to,' she replied honestly, 'but your papa chased my monster away, too.'

'Papa's the best,' Ianthe stated with a degree of adoration in her voice that tugged at Anna's heart. She remembered a time when she'd believed that her father was the most wonderful person in the world, and her feeling of devastation when he'd walked out and left her behind.

Damon was nothing like her father, she acknowledged. He would never abandon his child. It was a week since she had arrived in Greece and discovered that the modelling assignment for Tina Theopoulis had partly been a trick to lure her to Damon's home. In that time she had quickly come to realise that Damon's daughter was a happy, well-adjusted child who was utterly confident of her father's love.

Ianthe would always be Damon's first priority and Anna admired and respected him for his dedication to his daughter. She would never be jealous of his love for his little girl. But the ghost of his dead wife was another matter.

'Are you going to have a very *long* shower?' Ianthe asked in a tone that told Anna she was struggling to hide her impatience.

'Five minutes max,' Anna assured her. 'Where is your papa?'

'Waiting on the terrace. I'll tell him you're almost ready.' Ianthe bounded out of the room and threw a final plea over her shoulder. '*Hurry up,* Anna!'

Ten minutes later Anna had managed to shower, blow-dry her hair and slip into a pair of white jeans and lemon yellow strap top. If she was honest, she was almost as excited about the coming trip as Ianthe and she quickly applied the minimum of make-up and sprayed her wrists with her favourite perfume before heading for the lift.

She had spent the first few days since Damon's revelation that Philip Stone was dead in a state of shock. It was hard to accept that the man who had caused her such misery and mental anguish was gone for good.

Even though she hadn't seen her stepfather for years, the idea that he was still enjoying his disgusting fantasises about her had filled her with revulsion. Damon's news had created a heady sense of relief. She felt as though she had been released from a life sentence, and the mental barriers that had prevented her from having a sexual relationship were slowly disappearing.

As the week had progressed she'd realised that the past was finally buried and she could look to the future with a new optimism. The thought of making love with Damon no longer filled her with fear. Indeed, every time he kissed her she responded with an eager passion that she hoped would show him that she was ready for them to become lovers.

But to her frustration he had made no move to take her to bed. At first she'd thought that the gentle sensitivity he'd shown her all week was his way of giving her time to come to terms with the news of her stepfather's death. He was obviously determined not to rush her, she decided, when each night he escorted her to her room and kissed her until she was senseless with longing, before politely bidding her good night and retreating to his own room.

However, as the days and nights slipped past her doubts grew and she wondered if his seeming reluctance to deepen their relationship was for another reason. Damon's wife was dead, but her memory lived on. Every room in the villa was adorned with her artwork—vibrantly beautiful paintings and exquisite sculptures that were a lasting legacy to Eleni's incredible talent.

How tragic that the pretty and gifted young woman pictured in the photographs that Ianthe had proudly shown her had died so young, and when she'd had so much to live for, Anna brooded. She didn't doubt that Damon had been deeply in love with his wife, and in Ianthe—who was the image of her mother—he had a visual reminder of all that he had lost.

Eleni was a hard act for any woman to follow and she had no intention of even trying, she accepted when she reached the terrace and saw Damon sitting beneath the shade of the pergola. He'd even admitted that he wasn't looking for another wife. But as her senses flared at the sight of him she wondered if she could cope with a brief affair and emerge unscathed.

'Good morning, Anna—did you sleep well?'

Damon lowered his newspaper and subjected her to a slow appraisal that brought a flush of colour to her cheeks. Although she was one of the most photographed women in the world, her self-confidence was shaky and she couldn't help thinking that she must look pale and uninteresting compared to Eleni's exotic beauty.

'Too well, I'm afraid,' she murmured apologetically. For the first time in years she was able to sleep without fear of the nightmares that had so often plagued her. 'I had no idea it was so late, but I'm ready now,' she added with a smile when she watched Ianthe hop impatiently from foot to foot.

'Good—we'll leave as soon as you've had breakfast.'

'Oh, I'm not hungry,' she said quickly.

'Well, we're not going anywhere until you've eaten, *pedhaki mou,*' Damon told her implacably. 'If you don't wish to disappoint Ianthe, I suggest you sit down and have some fruit and yoghurt.'

'Has anyone ever told you you're the bossiest man in the world?' Anna snapped as she took her place at the table and forced a smile for the maid who had set a cup of coffee in front of her.

'No one else has ever dared,' Damon admitted with one of the devastating smiles that took her breath away. 'Trust you to break the mould, Anna *mou.*'

The note of gentle affection in his voice, teamed with the warmth in his eyes, made her heart lurch and she hastily tore her gaze from him and helped herself to a selection of fresh fruit.

In faded denims that clung lovingly to his thighs, and a black T-shirt stretched taut over his broad chest, he was awesome. Anna was filled with a crazy urge to lean across the table, snatch his newspaper out of his hands and claim his mouth with her own, in a kiss that would leave him in no doubt of what she wanted.

Now was not the time, she conceded—and with Ianthe present, certainly not the place. She forced herself to swallow a segment of orange but when she dared to glance up again she was shocked by the stark hunger in Damon's eyes before his expression was hidden behind the veil of his thick black lashes.

His heart might belong to Eleni, but he could not disguise his desire for *her.* The knowledge caused liquid heat to course through Anna's veins and she was conscious that her breasts had tightened so that her nipples strained against her thin cotton top. If she had any sense, she would refuse to go to his farmhouse retreat on Poros and instead catch the next flight home. But when had good sense ever triumphed over love? she brooded grimly.

After weeks of desperately trying to ignore her feelings, she could no longer deny the truth. She loved Damon with an intensity that terrified her and, although she knew she should leave while her heart was still intact, the thought of walking away from him was unbearable. Besides, she reassured herself, there was Ianthe to consider.

From the moment Damon had introduced her to his daughter, she'd felt an immediate bond with the little girl. She'd still been reeling from Damon's shocking revelation that Philip Stone was dead, her emotions had been raw, and the innocence of Ianthe's smile had brought home to her the loss of her own childhood at the hands of her stepfather.

She would do everything in her power to protect this child, she realised. But the fact that Ianthe had come to mean so much to her in such a short space of time was something of a shock, and she was aware of an ache of maternal longing that six months ago would have astounded her.

'Would you like another slice of melon, Anna?' Ianthe's voice broke into her thoughts.

'No, thank you, I've had enough breakfast, and I'm sure you've had enough of waiting for me. Shall we see if we can persuade your papa to take us on his boat now?' Anna gave the little girl a conspiratorial wink and pushed her empty bowl towards Damon.

'Satisfied?' she queried.

'Not yet, *pedhaki mou,* but I live in hope,' he replied softly, the gleam in his eyes sending liquid heat scalding through her veins.

He was the Devil's own, she decided as she jumped to her feet, praying that Ianthe would not comment on her scarlet cheeks. But, dear God, she couldn't resist his smouldering sexual promise for much longer and perhaps on Poros— away from this house that was a shrine to his dead wife— she wouldn't have to.

Three days later Anna was willing to believe that she had died and gone to heaven. The island of Poros was a green paradise set in an azure blue sea, and yet it was little more than an hour's boat ride away from noisy, bustling Athens. Damon's holiday retreat was a rustic farmhouse that clung to a hillside and commanded spectacular views over the island and the sea beyond.

Anna loved the simplicity of the house, which was comfortable but basic, with cool stone floors and whitewashed walls. Unlike the villa in Athens, there were no staff at the farmhouse and she enjoyed the intimacy of helping Damon to prepare their meals while Ianthe set the rough wooden table with cutlery and napkins, and a vase of wild flowers that she had collected.

Playing at families was better than she could ever have anticipated, Anna acknowledged—but playing was all it was. In another few days they would return to Athens. Damon could not take time away from his business indefinitely, and neither could she. There were assignments booked for Australia and the Far East, commitments she must honour, and it was ridiculous to wish for time to stand still so that she could live here with Damon for ever.

With a sigh, she closed her book and rolled over onto her stomach. She had spent the morning on the beach with Ianthe, while Damon put in a couple of hours' work on his laptop. The heat of the midday sun was making her feel sleepy, the sound of the waves lapping the shore hypnotic.

'I hope you're wearing plenty of sunscreen?' A familiar voice sounded in her ear while at the same time something cold hit her back. Uttering a yelp of surprise, she opened her eyes to find Damon kneeling beside her with a bottle of lotion in his hands.

'I can do it myself,' she muttered breathlessly as her senses leapt into vibrant life at the feel of his hands on her sun-warmed skin.

'But you don't have to, *pedhaki mou,* when I'm happy to do it for you,' Damon said equably. 'Hold still, I don't want to get cream on your bikini.' He deftly released the clasp of her bikini top and Anna buried her face in her arms to stifle a groan when he began to massage cream into her skin.

'Damon!'

He splayed his fingers on her back and then over her ribcage until he reached the soft swell of her breast. For a few mindless seconds she was tempted to turn over so that he could cup her breasts fully in his big hands. Maybe he would stroke his fingers across her nipples, or even push her bikini aside to take one engorged peak into his mouth.

Heat pooled between her thighs. She felt hot with desire. Did he have any idea what he was doing to her? She opened her eyes and noted the savage hunger in his with an element of satisfaction. This desperate longing was not hers alone. The sexual chemistry that had smouldered between them since their arrival on Poros was at combustion point, but this was a public beach and Ianthe was about.

'It's hell, isn't it?' Damon murmured in a matter of fact voice that was at variance with the slumberous sensuality of his gaze. He refastened her bikini with hands that shook slightly. 'I'm just thankful that the sea is so cold. As you may have noticed, Anna *mou,* I spend a lot of time in it, trying to exorcise my more basic desires.'

Anna sat up and calmly met his gaze. The patience and sensitivity he'd shown her since she'd confided in him about her stepfather was humbling. He would never hurt her—or not physically, at any rate. Emotionally was a different matter. He didn't love her and never would, but he cared for her, she would swear by it. She meant more to him than his previous mistresses. The very fact that he had introduced her to Ianthe and the rest of his family was proof of that.

He had sworn that he would not rush her, and even here on Poros, where they had spent every waking minute of each day consumed with a blistering awareness of each other, he was still waiting for her to give him some sign that she was ready to take their relationship to a physical level.

She stared at his face, noting the slant of his heavy brows, the strong nose and the sensual curve of his mouth. Love had caught her unawares and trapped her in its silken web. She didn't want to love him. She'd spent her life vowing that she would never repeat the mistakes her mother had made and leave herself open to the anguish of rejection. But love, she had discovered, had a will of its own.

If she walked away from him now, she would leave her heart behind. She had spent the years since she'd left home meticulously planning every aspect of her life, until Damon had crashed into it. He had torn down her defences, but she was no longer afraid to admit that she needed him.

He would be her first and only lover. How could any other man come close to him? It was time to be daring, to live for the here and now and stop looking to the future where almost inevitably, one day, they would part.

Acting on impulse, she swung her legs round so that she was kneeling on the sand in front of him and gave him an impish smile. 'I can think of several other ways of exorcising those desires, Damon,' she told him softly. 'And none of them involve swimming in the cold sea.'

For a moment he stiffened and she watched the way his broad chest heaved with the effort of drawing air into his lungs. 'Would you care to elaborate, *pedhaki mou?*'

He had lowered his head so that his mouth hovered millimetres from hers and, uttering a low cry, she closed the space between them to claim his lips in a kiss that pierced his soul. For the first time Anna held nothing back. She wanted no more doubts or misunderstandings and she responded to the tentative sweep of his tongue by parting her lips and drawing him into her.

Passion ripped through them with the ferocity of a flame set to tinder. She heard Damon mutter something in Greek before his arms closed around her and he dragged her up against the solid wall of his chest. One hand tangled in her hair while the other roamed up and down her spine, forcing her hips into burning contact with his so that she was made achingly aware of the power of his arousal.

Finally, when she didn't think she could withstand much more without dragging him down onto the sand and begging him to take her, he eased the pressure of his mouth on hers until the kiss was a gentle caress on her swollen lips.

'Are you sure, Anna?' he demanded rawly, the huskiness of his tone warning her of his tenuous hold on his self-control. 'We don't have to rush. I'm prepared to wait—'

'But I'm not,' she interrupted him softy, placing her finger across his lips. 'I want you, Damon. When you encouraged me to talk about what happened with my stepfather, and then revealed that he can no longer hurt me, or any other vulnerable young girl—you set me free. I no longer feel dirty or ashamed. I feel beautiful, not because of my life in front of the camera, but because you make me feel beautiful. I want to thank you,' she whispered. She linked her arms around his neck but Damon gripped her wrists.

'You don't have to thank me—certainly not like this,' he told her fiercely, his eyes so dark that she thought she would drown in their depths. 'When we make love, I want it to be because you are *hungry* with desire for me, not because you feel you owe me the pleasure of your body to repay a debt.'

The raw emotion in his gaze made her heart clench with love. Even now, when his big, powerful body was trembling with need for her, he was still determined to protect her. She had to bite her lip to prevent herself from spilling out how much he meant to her and instead she ran her hand over his chest, following the path of dark hairs that arrowed over his stomach, until she reached the waistband of his shorts.

'I'm hungry now, Damon,' she whispered provocatively and heard him growl deep in his throat. His face was a taut mask, desire etched onto every sharp angle and plane, but instead of taking up the invitation of her soft lips he reached out and smoothed her hair back from her temple.

'Your timing leaves a lot to be desired, Anna *mou*,' he teased gently. Ianthe's voice drifted towards them on the breeze and Anna watched as the desire in his gaze slowly faded and was replaced with rueful amusement.

'When are we having lunch, Papa? I'm starving,' Ianthe announced as she threw herself down on the sand, blithely unaware of the simmering tension in the air.

'Me, too,' Damon murmured beneath his breath so that only Anna heard the heartfelt words. Suddenly the sun seemed to shine brighter and the sea was a more intense blue. Her senses were acutely aware of the salt tang in the air, the mew of a seagull circling above them and the lambent warmth in Damon's eyes.

'There's plenty of time,' she whispered, feeling as though her heart would burst when he lifted her hand to his mouth and grazed his lips across her knuckles.

'All the time in the world,' he promised with a smile that filled her with joy and a tiny flame of hope that she could actually mean something to him.

After lunch they took the boat out on a leisurely cruise around the island before mooring in a tiny, deserted cove where Ianthe could swim to her heart's content. They returned to the farmhouse as the sun was setting and Anna showered and changed into a delicate chiffon dress with narrow shoulder straps and a tiered skirt in soft shades of green. The colour looked good against her golden tan and she felt a thrill of feminine pleasure when she stood back to inspect her reflection.

The sun had lightened her hair to platinum blonde and she caught it up in a loose knot on top of her head, leaving a few tendrils to frame her face. A coat of mascara to darken her lashes and a touch of pink gloss on her lips was the only make-up she needed, and she was spraying perfume on her pulse points when there was a tap on her door.

'You look…exquisite.' Damon paused in the doorway, unable to hide his reaction to her as streaks of colour ran along the sharp line of his cheekbones. She had never seen him looking anything other than supremely self-confident and the realisation that he too could be feeling vulnerable and unsure tore at her heart.

'Thank you—you're looking pretty good yourself. Almost good enough to eat,' she added, her eyes dancing with mischief and another emotion that made Damon long to forget dinner and simply draw her into his arms.

'Hold that thought,' he bade her urgently. 'I thought just the two of us could go out tonight. The family in the beach-front house are old friends who are happy for Ianthe to stay with them for a couple of hours.'

'Have you asked Ianthe what she'd like to do?' Anna walked over to him and calmly met his gaze. 'I know she will always be the most important person in your life, Damon. It's as it should be and I wouldn't want it any other way. I certainly don't want her to feel that I'm pushing her out. I know how that feels,' she added huskily. 'I think it would be nice if we all dined out together.'

'You take my breath away, do you know that?' he replied quietly, his eyes darkening with admiration. 'You suffered a hellish childhood, but instead of being bitter and resentful you spend much of your time and energy raising money for children's charities. You have incredible patience with my daughter and I thank you, *pedhaki mou.*' He dropped a brief, tantalising kiss on her mouth and moved towards the door. 'I'd better tell Ianthe to get changed. She's been desperate for an opportunity to wear her new dress.'

They ate in a little taverna overlooking the harbour. Anna had dined in exclusive restaurants around the world, but she'd never enjoyed a meal more than in the friendly ambience of the family-run taverna.

Conscious of Ianthe's presence, she kept her conversation with Damon light and innocuous, but she was aware of the far more intimate message in his eyes and her excitement grew. Tonight she would give herself to him completely. The thought no longer filled her with fear, but a heady sense of anticipation that made her eyes sparkle and brought a flush of rosy colour to her cheeks.

'Would you like more wine?' he asked towards the end of the meal.

'I'd better not; it makes me sleepy.'

'Definitely not in that case—I want you wide awake and conscious of every kiss and stroke and lick and bite when I make love to you.'

'Damon!' Anna gasped. Ianthe had jumped down from the table and was watching the boats bobbing in the harbour, but she was afraid the little girl might overhear. 'You're embarrassing me.'

'I hope not,' he replied, suddenly serious. 'There is nothing embarrassing or disgusting about the act of love, *pedhaki mou.* I want to honour you with my body and give you more pleasure than you've ever known.'

His words caused a delicious shiver to run the length of Anna's spine and she moistened her suddenly dry lips with her tongue. 'Right—actually, shall we go? Ianthe seems to have finished and I couldn't eat another thing,' she said hurriedly, trying to ignore Damon's soft chuckle.

They walked hand in hand back across the beach while Ianthe ran on ahead, laughing as she dodged the waves.

'Straight up to bed, young lady,' Damon bade his daughter when they reached the farmhouse. 'Say good night to Anna.'

In reply, Ianthe wrapped her arms around Anna's waist and squeezed. 'I'm glad you're here, Anna. We're having a lovely time, aren't we?'

'We certainly are,' Anna agreed. 'Good night, darling, I'll see you in the morning.'

Damon followed Ianthe up the narrow stairs to her bedroom in the eaves. The master bedroom and guest room were on the floor below and Anna hesitated on the landing, her heart thudding in her chest as she debated which room to enter, before she made her decision.

Ten minutes later Damon found her in his room, staring out over the bay where the moonlight dappled the sea with silvery fingers. 'She was asleep the moment her head touched the pillow,' he murmured.

'I'm not surprised after all the swimming she's done today.' A little of Anna's tension eased and she smiled fondly at the thought of the child whom she was quickly growing to love. She was aware of Damon crossing the room to slide his arms around her waist and draw her up against his chest. He trailed a line of kisses along her neck and she gasped when she felt him nip her earlobe.

'You see, I told you biting can be pleasurable,' he teased. He turned her in his arms and trapped her gaze, the gentle warmth in his eyes demolishing her nerves. 'I understand the legacy of fear your stepfather inflicted on you and you have my word that I won't demand more of you than you are prepared to give,' he promised. 'The moment you want me to stop, just say so, Anna.'

His mouth hovered above hers, tantalisingly close. She wasn't worried about him stopping, she just wanted him to start, Anna thought desperately as she wound her arms around his neck. 'Just kiss me, Damon,' she muttered, and he needed no further encouragement.

He captured her mouth and initiated a sensual exploration that left her in no doubt of his hunger for her. Helplessly she tipped her head back and welcomed the thrust of his tongue between her lips while he dragged her hard up against his thighs and made her aware of the throbbing power of his arousal.

Slowly he slid the strap of her dress over her shoulder, followed by the other, and then peeled the material down to reveal her breasts. Anna could not repress a shiver when he cupped each soft mound in his palms and held her breath when he delicately stroked his thumb pads over her tight nipples.

Sensation flooded through her and she moaned when he trailed his lips over the pulse that was beating frantically at the base of her throat, down, down until finally he was where she wanted him to be. The stroke of his tongue sent pleasure spiralling through her and she clutched his hair and held his head against her breast while he took her nipple into his mouth.

By the time he had metered the same exquisite punishment on its twin, she was trembling so much that her legs could barely support her. Damon must have sensed it and he swept her into his arms and carried her over to the bed where he carefully laid her on the cool sheets.

Anna watched, wide-eyed, when he unbuttoned his shirt. The sun had darkened his skin to bronze and the hard muscles of his abdomen rippled beneath the covering of wiry black hairs when he shrugged the shirt over his shoulders and dropped it to the floor. He paused fractionally and then moved his hand to the zip of his trousers.

Anna swallowed but could not drag her eyes from him as the trousers joined his shirt and he stood before her, his silk boxers struggling to conceal the jutting length of his manhood.

'Are you afraid of me, Anna?' he queried huskily.

Slowly she shook her head. She was awed, yes. Slightly apprehensive of what was to come, especially when faced with the magnificent proof of how much he desired her. But she did not fear him.

Silently she opened her arms and he moved towards the bed. When he tugged the folds of her dress down, she obligingly lifted her hips, although she hesitated when he hooked his fingers in the waistband of her knickers. He held her gaze as he slowly drew them over her silky smooth thighs, and only when he felt that he had her full confidence did he allow his eyes to move over her naked beauty.

'You are so very lovely, Anna *mou*,' he muttered when he joined her on the bed and claimed her mouth in kiss that quickly became a sensual feast. Anna twisted restlessly beneath him when he trailed a moist path across each breast before sliding lower, over her flat stomach where he paused to dip his tongue into her navel.

The sensations he aroused were new and faintly shocking, and she felt liquid heat pool between her thighs. She inhaled sharply when his dark head moved lower still. Surely he wouldn't...?

He would, and did—gently nudging her legs apart so that he could use his tongue in the most intimate caress she had ever experienced. Anna cried out and frantically tugged his hair, trying to make him stop.

It felt so good. She had never believed it possible to feel such intense pleasure and after a moment she let go of his hair and dug her fingers into his shoulders as if she needed to anchor herself to something solid. She remembered his

teasing comments about licking her. Dear God, she had
never expected that he would use his tongue quite so
thoroughly.

But her ability to think rationally was disappearing
beneath the waves of sensation that were building inexorably,
causing her to arch her hips in mute supplication for him to
continue his mastery. The ache inside her overwhelmed any
other consideration and demolished any lingering fears that
her stepfather had induced. She wanted Damon deep inside
her. Only he could appease her desperate need.

With a cry of frustration she reached down and sought to
drag his boxers over his hips. She wanted to feel him push
against her without the barrier of fine silk. But as he moved
slightly to aid her a sharp, high-pitched scream shattered the
sexual haze that enveloped them.

'Ianthe!' Damon muttered a savage curse in his own
tongue and sat up, dragging air into his lungs. Never in his
life had he resented his adored daughter, but right now he
would happily ignore her fearful cry.

'Papa, Papa, come quickly!'

'I'll have to go to her,' he said harshly as he forced himself
to get up from the bed and move away from the temptation
of Anna's long, slender limbs that only moments before he
had imagined her wrapping around him. 'She's probably had
a nightmare.'

Ianthe screamed again and Anna's blood ran cold. She remembered what it felt like to wake in the night, heart
pumping with fear as demons haunted her. Something had
plainly terrified the little girl and they couldn't leave her.

She swung her legs over the side of the bed, suddenly
acutely conscious of her nakedness. Damon had pulled on
a robe and she hastily reached for his shirt to cover herself.
'Of course you must go,' she assured him as Ianthe's sobs
echoed through the house. 'I'll get her a drink.'

When she entered the attic bedroom a few minutes later, she found Ianthe huddled on the bed and Damon half under it.

'Spider,' he answered her silent query when he lifted his head.

'Have you caught it, Papa?' Ianthe asked tearfully.

'Not yet, *kyria*. I think it's run away. It's probably deaf,' he added, struggling to hide his impatience.

'I don't want to go to sleep when it's under my bed.' More tears fell and he groaned.

'I'll get the torch and have another look,' he muttered and strode out of the bedroom, leaving Anna to deal with Ianthe.

'It was that big,' the little girl assured Anna seriously, spreading her hands to demonstrate the size of the creature. 'I hate spiders and I want to go home.'

Following her natural instincts, Anna wrapped her arms around the sobbing child and gently rocked her until she began to relax. 'I'm sure it's gone now, darling. Let's think about all the lovely things we're going to do tomorrow.' The ploy worked and she watched in satisfaction as Ianthe's eyes grew heavy while she planned the next day's activities.

'Are you feeling better now?' she queried softly. She pulled the sheet up to Ianthe's chin and stroked her curls. 'You don't really want to go home, do you? You love it here on Poros.'

The child gave a sleepy nod. 'Papa loves it here, too. Poros is his favourite place in the whole world—that's why he brought my mama here for their honeymoon. Do you think she liked it here, Anna?'

'I'm sure she did,' Anna replied quietly, fighting to control the sudden feeling of nausea that had swept over her. Unlike at the villa in Athens, there were none of Eleni's paintings or sculptures in the farmhouse. The lack of visual reminders of Damon's first wife was one reason why she had felt so relaxed here, Anna acknowledged sickly. It was a shock to discover that the farmhouse itself was a shrine to Eleni's memory and the love that Damon had once shared with her.

Ianthe had fallen back to sleep and she tiptoed out of the room to bump into Damon on the landing.

'Sorry I was so long—I couldn't find the damn torch.'

'It's all right. Ianthe's gone to sleep now—and I'd like to do the same.' She could not bring herself to meet his gaze and stared determinedly at the floor. She heard him sigh and sensed the moment he reached out to touch her. *'Don't, please…I can't:…not now,'* she pleaded. 'I just want to go to bed—alone.'

'Of course.' Damon's tone was politely neutral but his expression was grim. 'I'm sorry, Anna, but the reality of having a child is that sometimes they need you at the most inopportune moments.'

She paused in the doorway to her room and stared at him. 'I appreciate that.'

'Do you? Are you sure you're not punishing me for putting the concerns of my daughter over you?' he demanded bitterly. 'Because, like it or not, that's the way it has to be. I thought you were different. I thought you understood.'

'I do,' Anna cried, but her words were drowned out by the sound of Damon slamming his bedroom door savagely behind him.

CHAPTER ELEVEN

'Anna—over here, sweetheart! Give us a smile. Have you got anything to say regarding the rumours about you and the pop star Mitch Travis?'

Anna flicked the photographer an icy stare, guaranteed to freeze even the most determined members of the press pack who were tailing her through Sydney Airport. She was dressed head to toe in designer clothes. Her face was exquisitely made up—her lips coated in a chic pale gloss while her hair was swept up into a severe knot on top of her head. The finished effect was as she had intended; an elegant, aloof Ice Princess who would never reveal to the paparazzi that her heart was breaking.

At the check-in desk she subjected the hapless reporter to a final look of haughty disdain before sweeping into the departure lounge, followed by her entourage of assistants. The past three weeks in Australia had been hell, which was in no way the fault of the vast continent or its people, she conceded grimly.

She would give anything to be back on Poros with Damon, but after their acrimonious parting it was unlikely that he would ever want to see her again.

She had spent the remainder of the night after Ianthe had disturbed them torn between a desperate desire to knock on

Damon's bedroom door and wrestling with the bitter knowledge that she could never compete with the ghost of his dead wife.

Poros would always be a special place for her and Damon—or so she'd believed—a paradise island where they had spent precious time together and first consummated their relationship. Except that they hadn't.

It had hurt immeasurably to discover that he had done it all before. No doubt he had once eaten in the taverna by the harbour with Eleni, and together they would have explored the many coves and beaches of the island. Had he made love to his wife for the first time in the master bedroom of the farmhouse? The same bed where *she* had been so eager to give herself to him. Perhaps he had even been thinking about his honeymoon night while he'd made love to her, and imagined that it was Eleni he was holding in his arms.

Jealousy was a corrosive poison that had scarred much of her mother's life. She could not allow it to ruin hers. If she felt this bad about a ghost, how would she cope when Damon's attention began to stray?

It would kill her, she had accepted bleakly. She loved him so much that the idea of him even looking at another woman would destroy her and she would become clingy and obsessive, just as her mother had been. Walking away from him now, while she still had the strength of will, was the only answer.

But when she had broken the untruth the following morning, that the date of her assignment in Australia had been brought forward, Damon had not bothered to hide his anger.

'You can't just leave,' he hissed furiously, conscious that Ianthe was in earshot. 'Whatever the reason for your change of heart, between the time you were a wild temptress in my arms, and now, I won't let you go.'

'You can't stop me,' she replied, closing her heart to the silent plea in his eyes. 'This is work, Damon, my career, which will always be my first priority, as Ianthe is yours.'

'Is that what this is all about?' he asked scathingly. 'You resent the fact that I have a child now that you've spent time with us and discovered the reality of parenthood.'

'I do not. That's a foul thing to say. I know how much you love her and I…I'm fond of her, too.'

'Then why are you so determined to hurt her? Because you're not just leaving Poros, are you, Anna? You're leaving me for good and running out on our relationship.'

'In all honesty, how can we have a relationship?' Anna flung at him. 'The most we could hope for is a brief fling when our hectic schedules happen to coincide. I don't want to live like that, Damon, and that's why I've decided to end it now.'

For a moment he'd seemed totally stunned. His face was ashen and the torment in his eyes sowed the first seeds of doubt in Anna's mind. Maybe he did care. Maybe she'd got it wrong. 'Do you have any other suggestions?' she asked quietly, knowing that it was ridiculous to wish for some indication of commitment from him, but wishing anyway.

'You could give up modeling, for a start, or at least cut down on your assignments. You don't need to work, *pedhaki mou*. I will take care of you,' he murmured, sliding his arms around her waist and drawing her close.

For an infinitesimal second Anna was tempted to lay her head on his chest and give in—allow him to take over her life. She knew he would do as he said. No doubt he would install her in an elegant Athens apartment, conveniently close to his own home, where he would visit several times a week—perhaps even pop in during his lunch hour for a quickie, she thought cynically. Common sense quickly reasserted itself and she stepped away from him.

'That's your idea of a compromise? I give up everything that I've worked for and you give up what, exactly? I'm sorry, Damon, but I will never give up my career or my financial independence for any man, even you.'

He gave up then, his face seemingly hewn from stone while she bade a heart-wrenching farewell to Ianthe and evaded the issue of when she would be coming back. He was silent on the trip to the harbour but as she was about to step onto the ferry he caught hold of her shoulder and spun her round, sliding a hand beneath her chin to force her to look at him.

'This is not over, Anna,' he told her fiercely. 'I don't know what you want from me. I suspect you don't even know yourself. But when you've worked it out, I'll be waiting for you.'

He swooped before she had time to react, capturing her mouth in a savage, possessive kiss that demanded her response. Anna clung to him helplessly, while her heart splintered into a thousand shards. How could she tell him that she knew exactly what she wanted from him, when it was the one thing he could not give?

His heart belonged to the beautiful, gifted Greek girl who had given birth to his precious daughter. He had chosen Eleni for his wife and even now, years after her death, he surrounded himself with her artwork as if he could not bear to let her go.

She would only ever be a poor second, Anna acknowledged despairingly. And although she loved him more than life—that was something she could not bear.

The flight to Paris seemed to last for ever. Anna was thankful that she was able to travel in business class, which offered a degree of comfort and room to stretch her long legs. First class travel was one of the many perks of her job but over the last three weeks she'd concluded that she would even be prepared to sacrifice her precious career, if only Damon loved her.

At the airport in Paris she collected a hire car and, having left the city, spent a frustrating few hours trying to negotiate the narrow roads of rural northern France in search of her mother's remote *gîte*. Dusk was falling by the time she pulled up in a small courtyard and stared at the farmhouse that her mother shared with her third husband.

Damon had said that Charles Aldridge was a decent man, and for Judith's sake she hoped he was right, Anna thought as she eased her tired body out of the car. She didn't understand this sudden urgency to see her mother. They hadn't been close for years but she was falling apart and she needed someone to salvage the splinters of her heart.

'Anna! What are you doing here? Not that you're not welcome, of course,' Judith Christiansen—now Aldridge— babbled when she opened the door. 'It's so wonderful to see you, darling. I'd almost given up hope that you would ever visit.' She caught hold of Anna's hand and led her into the house. 'You must meet Charles. He's still working in the garden—I'll just call him.'

Judith turned and gave Anna a joyous smile. 'I suppose that lovely man of yours brought you. He promised he would try and persuade you to visit. Where is he?' As she glanced expectantly at the door Anna frowned.

'Which man?'

'Damon, of course,' her mother replied in a tone that suggested there could be no other man in Anna's life. 'He was so concerned about you when he visited a month or so ago. And he was so sympathetic when I explained about my divorce from your father. He seemed to understand how much it had affected you.' She stared in bemusement at the tears that were streaming down Anna's cheeks. 'What is it, darling?

Have you rowed? I'm sure you can sort it out. Damon loves you very much.'

'He doesn't,' Anna wept, unable to hide her inner anguish any longer. 'He's still in love with his first wife. His house is full of mementoes of her and he even took me to the place where he spent his honeymoon. She was so beautiful and clever, and I can't compete with her memory.'

'Don't be silly. I don't believe you have to compete with anyone,' Judith told her firmly as she put an arm around her shoulders and hugged her. 'I may not have been very successful in the choice of my first two husbands—this may come as a shock, but Philip Stone wasn't the charming man I first thought,' she confided, unaware of the shaft of pain that crossed Anna's face. 'But I do know love when I see it. And I saw it in Damon's eyes when he spoke of you,' she assured Anna firmly.

'Now, come and have something to eat. You're much too thin—I don't suppose you've been eating properly. After that you can have a bath and bed and in the morning you'll see that whatever has happened is just a lovers' tiff. I don't know anything about Damon's first wife, but I'm quite certain that you're the woman he loves now.'

Anna stood in the middle of the kitchen and buried her face in her hands. 'I think I may have made a terrible mistake,' she whispered. 'But I'm so afraid of becoming jealous and possessive like...' She halted abruptly so that her words hovered in the embarrassed silence.

'Like I was,' Judith finished the sentence for her. 'Oh, Anna, there are so many things I should have explained to you,' she said sadly. 'For most of my adult life I've suffered from a severe depressive illness, which thankfully is now controlled by medication. But for many years I struggled to deal with my feelings alone,' she admitted.

'There were times during your childhood when I was

paranoid and obsessive, and your father found it difficult to cope. The truth is, I drove Lars away, but it wasn't until all these years later, and thanks to Charles's wonderful support, that I've been able to accept that I was partly to blame for the collapse of my first marriage.'

Judith wiped her eyes with a hand that shook slightly. The betraying gesture tore at Anna's heart as for the first time she recognised her mother's fragility. She must have been an ideal target for Philip Stone—a vulnerable single mother with a young daughter in tow, Anna acknowledged bitterly.

The realisation lifted the resentment she had felt all these years, that her mother was in some way to blame for what had happened with her stepfather. Judith must have believed she was doing the best for her child by providing her with a father-figure—unaware that the man she had married was a monster. It would destroy her if she ever discovered how Anna had suffered at the hands of jolly Uncle Phil.

She would never tell her mother, Anna vowed. It was in the past and now Phil was dead and could no longer hurt anyone. Damon was the only person to know her secret and it was thanks to him that she had finally overcome the fears her stepfather had instilled in her.

Damon had shown her nothing but patience and incredible sensitivity but she had thrown it back in his face.

'I have to go to Greece,' she muttered dazedly. She didn't know if it was love that Judith had seen in Damon's eyes, but suddenly she didn't care. The last three weeks without him had been so unutterably miserable that she was prepared to risk her pride by admitting how much she loved him.

Maybe he would always care for Eleni, but he couldn't make love to a memory.

'I'm sorry, Mum, but I can't stop. I promise to return soon though. I have to go back to Damon and...'

'And tell him you love him,' her mother agreed gently. 'I

suppose it's useless trying to persuade you to stay the night, so I'd better drive you to the airport.'

The offices of Kouvaris Construction were in the heart of Athens. Anna stepped out of the heat of the late-summer sunshine into the cool interior of the reception area. Her heart was beating in time with the staccato tap of her stiletto heels on the marble floor as she strode past the startled receptionist and into the lift.

She had already elicited from Damon's sister that he was at work and that his office was on the top floor. Tina had also warned that her brother's mood had been grim ever since he'd returned from Poros and suggested that Anna was the only person who could make him smile again.

Somehow that seemed unlikely, Anna brooded when the lift halted at the top floor. She had carefully planned what she wanted to say to him, but now the time was here and her confidence was draining away faster than water down a plug-hole.

Taking a deep breath, she smiled at the elegant woman who she guessed was Damon's secretary, and marched briskly towards his office. The woman said something in Greek that probably translated to Damon did not want to be disturbed, but Anna ignored the warning and pushed open the door.

He looked tired and curiously dejected, with no sign of his usual wonderful arrogance, she noted when she stared greedily at him, feeling her body's instinctive response to his raw masculinity. He must have heard the click of the door but did not bother to lift his head as he growled a terse comment in Greek.

'Hello, Damon.'

She didn't know what she had been expecting and was shocked at the look of savage pain in his eyes, before his thick lashes fell, concealing his emotions. For those few brief seconds she had looked into his heart and relief crashed over her, making her legs feel decidedly wobbly.

'Anna. What a…pleasant surprise,' he said coolly. 'Why are you here?'

It was typical of Damon to ignore social niceties and go straight for the kill, Anna acknowledged ruefully. 'Can't you guess?' she asked.

'I gave up trying to fathom the intricacies of your mind long ago. Why don't you just tell me and save time for both of us?' He leaned back in his chair and surveyed her boldly, as if he were a sultan inspecting his latest concubine.

Once Anna would have felt self-conscious, but now she calmly met his gaze. Her skirt was shorter than she normally wore, revealing her long, slender legs in their sheer black hose. She watched in fascination the stain of colour that ran along Damon's cheekbones when his eyes slid all the way down to her heels.

Desire, the fierce chemistry that had always existed between them, still glittered in his dark eyes. It was a start, she thought. Passion was as powerful an emotion as love and if necessary she would use it to tie him to her until he no longer knew where passion ended and love began.

She sauntered across the room, unfastening the buttons of her jacket as she went. 'Perhaps this will give you some clue as to why I'm here,' she murmured. She shrugged the jacket over her shoulders and let it slip to the floor. Beneath it she was wearing nothing but a black lacy bra that cupped the creamy swell of her breasts. She shook back her hair and heard Damon inhale sharply, although his expression remained impassive.

With slow deliberation she unzipped her skirt and wriggled her hips to ease its path down over her thighs. The whole concept of peeling off her layers of clothing was incredibly liberating. Damon had freed her from the belief that her body was somehow sinful. She was proud of her breasts and her narrow waist and her endlessly long legs, and from the heat in his gaze he appreciated every one of her feminine curves.

That appreciation was not mirrored in his voice. 'Very nice,' he drawled in a tone of supreme indifference. 'Your Aussie lover is a lucky boy.'

'Who?' Anna stared at him, plainly bemused.

'Midge, or whatever he calls himself. The insect with the long hair and bug eyes.'

'You mean Mitch Travis, lead singer of Australia's biggest pop group.' Anna shook her head as realisation dawned. 'You're jealous!'

Damon did not deign to reply but the fury in his gaze should have sent her running for cover.

'For your information, I happened to be standing next to Mitch at a film première and the press immediately concocted the story that we're having an affair. In my world, it happens all the time.'

'I do not like your world,' Damon growled, sounding very Greek.

'Nothing happened,' she assured him as joy bubbled within her. He was jealous. That had to mean something. 'The only man I'll ever want is you.'

She leaned forwards, caught hold of his tie and pulled him towards her, seeking his mouth with newfound confidence. For a few nerve-racking seconds he remained stiff and unyielding before he wrapped his arms around her and dragged her down onto his knee.

'Anna *mou*, I don't think I can take much more of this,' he groaned when he finally lifted his head to stare at her softly swollen mouth and the slumberous desire in her eyes. 'I love you—' the words were wrenched from his soul

'—more than I believed it possible to love another human being. But my need for you is tearing me apart.'

His face twisted with emotion and Anna traced a shaky hand over his jaw. 'But I thought…' She broke off as joy unfurled within her like the petals of a flower opening to the sun. 'Oh, Damon, I love you, too. With all my heart,' she vowed fiercely, her eyes glistening with the emotions she no longer had to hide.

'Then why did you leave me?' he groaned. 'That night on Poros when Ianthe was frightened by the spider, you were so cold and distant and I knew then that I was losing you. But I can't change the fact that I have a child.'

'I love Ianthe almost as much as I love you,' Anna assured him softly. She flushed shamefacedly. 'I could never resent her, but I found it hard to deal with the fact that you're still in love with her mother.'

'Ianthe told me that night that you had spent your honeymoon at the farmhouse on Poros,' she added.

'Did she?' Damon frowned. 'It's true that I took Eleni to Poros, but we stayed at a friend's villa on the other side of the island. I only bought the farmhouse a couple of years ago as somewhere to take Ianthe and I told her about the honeymoon because I think it's important for her to know as many details as possible about her mother.'

'Eleni died a long time ago,' he said quietly. 'For Ianthe's sake I will always remember her, which is why I have all her artwork on display in the villa. I loved her, yes,' he agreed, tightening his arms around Anna to foil her bid for escape. 'She was a sweet girl. We met soon after the death of my parents and I suppose I wanted to recreate a sense of family. But my sadness was for the loss of a young life and when I think of her now, it is with affection. You are the love of my life, *pedhaki mou*. Together with Ianthe you are my reason for living.'

He sought her mouth with tender passion that quickly developed to an inferno of desire. The last three weeks without him had been purgatory, Anna thought as she wound her arms around his neck and parted her lips to savour the wicked sorcery of his tongue.

'I am a man of action rather than words,' Damon growled as his glorious arrogance bounced back. 'I need to show you how much you mean to me before I explode!'

He stood and carried her over to a door on the other side of his office. 'Sometimes if I've been working late, I sleep here,' he told her when he nudged the door open with his shoulder and strode over to the bed. The room was functional rather than decorative and he gave her a rueful glance. 'It's not the most romantic venue for your first time, *pedhaki mou*. If you prefer, we could check into a hotel.'

'No time,' Anna muttered feverishly as she fumbled with his shirt buttons. 'I want you to make love to me now. I can't wait. And I have no intention of lying here admiring the décor.'

The undisguised hunger in her eyes was all the encouragement Damon needed to strip down to his boxers with record speed. He hesitated for a moment and trapped her gaze while his hand moved to the waistband.

'Please, I want to see you,' she whispered, wetting her dry lips with the tip of her tongue.

Her plea almost sent him over the edge and when he shrugged out of his underwear the solid length of his arousal jutted proudly forwards.

'You are so beautiful,' Anna whispered, her faint apprehension fading as she absorbed the latent power of his muscle bound body. He was her Greek god and she was impatient to feel him inside her. Already she could feel the flood of warmth between her thighs and when he stretched out beside her she drew his head down and initiated a kiss that stirred his soul.

He removed her bra with fingers that shook slightly and cradled her breasts with gentle reverence before lowering his head to anoint each nipple with his lips. Anna moaned and arched her back, silently pleading for more. She felt him skim his hand over her flat stomach to the tiny triangle of black lace and lifted her hips so that he could remove her knickers.

Her slender body was naked except for the sheer black stockings that contrasted starkly against her pale flesh. Damon muttered a harsh imprecation and traced the wide band of lace at the junction between her thighs before pushing her legs apart with an edge of roughness that warned of his urgent desire to push deep inside her.

Anna felt no fear, only pleasure when he stroked her and then gently eased his fingers into her to perform an erotic dance that made her tremble. Only when he was sure that she was completely relaxed did he slide his hands beneath her bottom to angle her in readiness to receive him. She felt his hard length rub against the opening to her vagina and stretched her legs wider, eager to be one with the one man who had captured her heart.

'I love you, Anna *mou*.' The words were torn from him as he slowly entered her and then paused when he felt the fragile barrier of her virginity. 'I don't want to hurt you,' he muttered hoarsely, his face a rigid mask as he sought to retain control.

'You won't. I trust you, my love,' she whispered and lifted her hips towards him, tensed for a second and dug her nails into his shoulders as her muscles stretched around him, then relaxed when he eased in deep and filled her.

He claimed her lips with the same tender passion with which he had claimed her body and began to move, slowly at first and then, when she learned his rhythm, faster, deeper so that the sensations he aroused in her grew ever more intense.

'Damon!' She called his name as the waves of pleasure built inexorably, taking her higher and higher until she was poised at the edge of some magical place that she had never known existed. The agonising tension that gripped her was suddenly and shatteringly released in a tumultuous wave of pleasure that seemed impossible to withstand.

In the recesses of her mind she heard Damon cry out, a harsh, feral sound so that she instinctively clung to him as his big body shuddered and he drove into her one last time.

Breathing hard, he rested his forehead against hers and felt the wetness on her cheeks. 'Are you all right?' he asked desperately.

'I love you.' She placed a finger over his lips and blinked away her tears.

'You know I'll never let you go? You'll have to marry me, *agape mou*. Please,' he added huskily when she stared at him with wide, stunned eyes. 'Make me the happiest man in the world? I know your career is important to you and I respect your choice to work, but perhaps you could be based in Athens rather than England. I admit that I'll hate it when you're away on assignments,' he added honestly, 'but I'll be waiting for you every time you come home.'

The last of Anna's lingering doubts disappeared and with it her old fear of not being financially dependent and she smiled at him. 'You didn't use protection, did you?'

'No,' he said slowly, frowning at the sudden change in conversation.

'And I'm not on the pill, so technically I could already be pregnant.'

'Technically I suppose you could.'

The glow of love in her eyes made him catch his breath.

'I think we should give Ianthe a little brother or sister as soon as possible, don't you?' she murmured, sliding her hand down to where their bodies were still joined. 'And if you leave me any spare time outside of the bedroom, I could always model maternity wear.'

'Be warned, *agape mou*,' he told her, his eyes darkening with desire as he stirred deliciously within her, 'I shall ensure that you have very little spare time!'

**Harlequin Presents brings you
a brand-new duet by star author**

Sharon Kendrick

THE GREEK BILLIONAIRES' BRIDES

Power, pride and passion—discover how only
the love and passion of two women can reunite
these wealthy, successful brothers,
divided by a bitter rivalry.

Available June 2008:

THE GREEK TYCOON'S
BABY BARGAIN

Available July 2008:

THE GREEK TYCOON'S
CONVENIENT WIFE

Don't miss the brilliant
new novel from

Natalie Rivers

**featuring a dark, dangerous
and decadent Italian!**

THE SALVATORE
MARRIAGE DEAL

Available June 2008
Book #2735

*Look out for more books
from Natalie Rivers coming soon,
only in Harlequin Presents!*

TALL, DARK AND SEXY

The men who never fail—seduction included!

Brooding, successful and arrogant, these men
can sweep any female they desire off her feet.
But now there's only one woman they want—
and they'll use their wealth, power, charm and
irresistibly seductive ways to claim her!

**Don't miss any of the titles in this exciting
collection available June 10, 2008:**

*Harlequin Presents EXTRA delivers a themed
collection every month featuring 4 new titles.*

REQUEST YOUR FREE BOOKS!

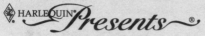 HARLEQUIN *Presents*

2 FREE NOVELS PLUS 2 FREE GIFTS!

YES! Please send me 2 FREE Harlequin Presents® novels and my 2 FREE gifts (gifts are worth about $10). After receiving them, if I don't wish to receive any more books, I can return the shipping statement marked "cancel". If I don't cancel, I will receive 6 brand-new novels every month and be billed just $4.05 per book in the U.S. or $4.74 per book in Canada, plus 25¢ shipping and handling per book and applicable taxes, if any*. That's a savings of close to 15% off the cover price! I understand that accepting the 2 free books and gifts places me under no obligation to buy anything. I can always return a shipment and cancel at any time. Even if I never buy another book, the two free books and gifts are mine to keep forever.   106 HDN ERRW 306 HDN ERRL

Name	(PLEASE PRINT)	
Address		Apt. #
City	State/Prov.	Zip/Postal Code

Signature (if under 18, a parent or guardian must sign)

Mail to the **Harlequin Reader Service:**
IN U.S.A.: P.O. Box 1867, Buffalo, NY 14240-1867
IN CANADA: P.O. Box 609, Fort Erie, Ontario L2A 5X3

Not valid to current subscribers of Harlequin Presents books.

Want to try two free books from another line?
Call 1-800-873-8635 or visit www.morefreebooks.com.

* Terms and prices subject to change without notice. N.Y. residents add applicable sales tax. Canadian residents will be charged applicable provincial taxes and GST. Offer not valid in Quebec. This offer is limited to one order per household. All orders subject to approval. Credit or debit balances in a customer's account(s) may be offset by any other outstanding balance owed by or to the customer. Please allow 4 to 6 weeks for delivery. Offer available while quantities last.

Your Privacy: Harlequin Books is committed to protecting your privacy. Our Privacy Policy is available online at www.eHarlequin.com or upon request from the Reader Service. From time to time we make our lists of customers available to reputable third parties who may have a product or service of interest to you. If you would prefer we not share your name and address, please check here. ☐

HP08R

I ♥ HARLEQUIN *Presents*

BROUGHT TO YOU BY FANS OF
HARLEQUIN PRESENTS.

We are its editors and authors
and biggest fans—and we'd
love to hear from YOU!

Subscribe today to our online blog at
www.iheartpresents.com

THE BOSS'S MISTRESS

Out of the office…and into his bed

These ruthless, powerful men are used
to having their own way in the office—
and with their mistresses they're also
boss in the bedroom!

**Don't miss any of our fantastic stories
in the July 2008 collection:**

#13 THE ITALIAN
TYCOON'S MISTRESS
by CATHY WILLIAMS

#14 RUTHLESS BOSS, HIRED WIFE
by KATE HEWITT

#15 IN THE TYCOON'S BED
by KATHRYN ROSS

#16 THE RICH MAN'S
RELUCTANT MISTRESS
by MARGARET MAYO

www.eHarlequin.com

HPE0708

HARLEQUIN *Presents*

EXTRA

Coming Next Month

Be sure to look out for our *Tall, Dark and Sexy* collection in Harlequin Presents EXTRA

#9 THE BILLIONAIRE'S VIRGIN BRIDE
Helen Brooks

#10 HIS MISTRESS BY MARRIAGE
Lee Wilkinson

#11 THE BRITISH BILLIONAIRE AFFAIR
Susanne James

#12 THE MILLIONAIRE'S MARRIAGE REVENGE
Amanda Browning

And Coming Next Month in Harlequin Presents

#2731 BOUGHT FOR REVENGE, BEDDED FOR PLEASURE
Emma Darcy
Ruthless

#2732 VIRGIN: WEDDED AT THE ITALIAN'S CONVENIENCE
Diana Hamilton
Innocent Mistress, Virgin Bride

#2733 THE BILLIONAIRE'S BLACKMAILED BRIDE Jacqueline Baird
Red-Hot Revenge

#2734 SPANISH BILLIONAIRE, INNOCENT WIFE Kate Walker
Latin Lovers

#2735 THE SALVATORE MARRIAGE DEAL Natalie Rivers
Expecting!

#2736 THE GREEK TYCOON'S BABY BARGAIN Sharon Kendrick
The Greek Billionaires' Brides

#2737 HIS MISTRESS BY ARRANGEMENT Natalie Anderson
Nights of Passion

#2738 MARRIAGE AT THE MILLIONAIRE'S COMMAND Anne Oliver
Taken by the Millionaire

Presents

She's cool, controlled…and ready to be claimed!

Supermodel Anneliese Christiansen seems to have it all—but Anna is an innocent, and has reasons for resisting Damon Kouvaris's ruthless seduction….

He's Mediterranean, made of money… and irresistibly marriageable!

Anna proves to be a challenge but Damon always gets what he wants…and if the prize is good enough he'll pay the price!

Will the Greek tycoon claim this virgin to be his bride…?

HARLEQUIN®
Presents®
Seduction and Passion Guaranteed

$4.75 U.S./$5.75 CAN.
ISBN-13:978-0-373-82081-8
ISBN-10:   0-373-82081-X

82081

0 65373 58604 9

Harlequin Presents® EXTR
www.eHarlequin.com